Reese Rivers Presents

Burn Butterfly Burn

Burn Butterfly Burn

Print Edition

Cover Art by:

Cat Cover Design

JUDE

Tate, Beck, and I are hanging out in the living room when the front door crashes open with a loud bang causing all three of us to jump to our feet. Ash barges in with a furious expression dragging with him, of all people, Savy's sister by the arm.

He shoves her towards us and rages out, "Your girl is a fucking liar! She's been lying to us all along!"

I roll my eyes at his dramatics, a grin tugging at my lips, already knowing what this is about. Somehow, he's finally figured out that Savy's his Butterfly and he's about to have a Charlie Sheen level meltdown.

"Pathetic little bookworm is actually the fucking Butterfly! She's been conning me for two fucking years!" He rages at us.

I shrug one shoulder and let my grin spread causing Ash to roar and lunge at me.

"You… you fucking knew?"

I bark a laugh as Tate and Beck pull him away from me. "I fucking told you to look harder, you blind dumbass!"

"Wait, Savy? Savy's the Butterfly?" Tate asks incredulously.

"Did NOT see that coming," Beck muses with a shocked look.

Ash rocks his head side to side in denial as everything he thought he knew goes up in smoke. I turn to look at the cunt he's dragged into our house and see the calculating look in her eyes as they bounce between us.

"What the fuck is she doing here?" I spit out.

Ash chokes out a bitter laugh. "Oh, it gets so much fucking worse! Her being the Butterfly is just the fucking tip of the iceberg when it comes to her lies." He reaches out and drags her forward. "Tell them! Fucking tell them who she really is!"

Vanessa tosses her hair back and a smug smile crosses her face. "My sister's real name is Savanna Sevan, as in…Sevan Stadium. She's worth billions! She could buy and sell each one of you. Her name is literally on the stadium you play football in! She's been making fools out of all of you this whole time!"

Whoa…that's…wow, just wow. My doll's loaded? That's…a lot to take in. I'm a little hurt that she didn't share that with me but she must have had a good reason to keep that to herself.

Movement behind the annoying blond has me tilting my head to the side to see past the screeching harpy and I see a white-faced Savy standing there. She's looking smoking hot in red stilettos, a black micro-mini, a sheer red crop top that shows a black bra underneath, and dark smoky made-up eyes with her hair billowing out around her. The long puffy jacket she must have thrown on over her Butterfly outfit is gaping open, showing me everything. She looks fucking bombing and I would love to see her dressed like that every day. The sister catches my look and spins around.

"There you are, sister! I was just letting your fuck-boys in on your little scam. I thought it was only fair to tell them that you're an heiress to billions and that you've been playing them all along."

Savy jerks her head as her mouth drops open to speak but her sister turns back to us and plows on viciously before she can say a word.

"She's not who she pretends to be! It's all a game to her. Savy acts like this lonely little nerd to suck guys in so she can play her sick and twisted games with them. She's done this before with other guys. She even managed to convince Hunter that she was a virgin! She's a slutty whore who will fuck anyone to satisfy her sick mind."

"No! I've never..." Savy tries to get out.

"She's an embarrassment to our family. She has mental issues. That's why we make her use her mother's maiden name. There were even rumors that she had something to do with her dad's accident!"

Savy goes paler as she sucks in a shocked breath at such a cruel thing for her sister to say. I'm just about done with this bullshit. I can see how bad the vile words are hurting my doll and I'm a step from dragging this bitch out by her hair when Savy speaks in a broken whisper.

"No, no, no, none of that..."

"She's a fucking fake! Everything about my sister is a fake and you are all fools for falling for it!" Vanessa screeches over Savy's words.

That breaks Ash's control causing him to take a menacing step toward her and roar, "Yes, she is! You are a fucking fake. Two fucking years you've been conning me! Everything that comes out of your mouth is a lie."

Savy shakes her head violently and her eyes look to Tate but he's just shaking his head with a look of disgust. Beck stares back at her with dead, flat eyes like he's daring her to try and deny what the sister is saying. A small trickle of doubt moves through me. I don't care about her dancing and as far as her last name goes, so what, but it's the other things, the fucking around with other guys, and playing twisted games that has me feeling a touch uncertain. So when her hurt, panic-filled eyes land on me, I can't help myself. I need to hear her deny it.

"You been playing me, doll?"

As soon as I ask that, I know I've fucked up. I should have believed in her, believed in us, because I see my baby doll shatter at my lack of faith in her. Like a switch goes off inside of her, everything that makes her my doll drains away until she's just an empty shell in front of us. Her hands drop to her sides limply, her whole body droops, her eyes - fuck me… her beautiful blue eyes go flat, empty, and lifeless. They move sluggishly to look at each one of us and then she slowly turns away and starts walking toward the front door. With one stupid fucking question, I wiped out everything she felt for me, for all of us.

Vanessa laughs loudly and gets in her final parting shot at her back.

"Oh, Savanna, I almost forgot…Happy Fucking Birthday!"

My eyes bug out at how much worse this really is when I hear that. It's her birthday, it's her fucking birthday and I remember Beck telling us that her dad died in that accident on her birthday. She stumbles in her heels and presses a hand to the wall to keep herself upright, sliding against it the rest of the way to the door like she can barely hold herself up from the pain we've inflicted on her and that's when I lose my everlasting shit and scream her name. I try to shove past Ash and Tate to go to her, to scoop her up and fix what we've broken but they grab me and hold me back.

"Just let her fucking go! She made her bed with all her lies," Ash spits out. My elbow comes up and clocks him in the face causing him to let me go and fall back with a grunt. Tate's easy to shake off after that and I run to the front door to try to salvage this clusterfuck. My chest is heaving as I scream her name into the falling snow when I see the red tail lights flash as a car turns the corner off our street and I know she's in it.

"FUUUUUCK!"

Tears gather in the corner of my eyes and I try to blame the cold wind and snow whirling around me but I know it's because of the pain we caused her.

I whip around baring my teeth as fury takes over, needing to lash out and make someone pay for what we've done to her and race back into the house. The three of them are arguing with each other over what they just learned while the object of my fury stands there with a self-satisfied smile on her face. I head right for her and love how her eyes go big and scared when she catches sight of my expression. She tries to back away from me but there's nowhere for her to go as I close in on her. My tatted fingers curl and grip her blond hair and I wrench her head down as I drag her over to the kitchen island and slam the side of her face to it.

"Jude! What the fuck are you doing?"

"Let her go, man. You don't want to do this!"

Even to my ears, my laugh sounds maniacal. "Oh, but I really, really do!" I call back over the girl's screams. I reach over the counter to the knife block and pull a fillet knife and bring it to her neck. Everyone shuts the fuck up at that move.

"Sick and twisted games. That's what you said she plays, right? Well, let's play our own game. We'll start with a twisted fact so you know just how serious I am right now. Ready? Listen closely…it only takes a pen of pigs eight minutes to strip and eat a human body leaving no trace behind. The body will never be found…get it?"

She makes a mewling whine full of fear but tries to nod her head that I'm pressing to the counter.

"Fucking *Christ,* Jude!"

"He's fucking lost it!"

And then Ash, "She's not worth it, brother. Savy's not worth destroying your life over."

I turn my head to meet his eyes and growl, "Wrong…fucking…answer."

Back to the game. "You get to say yes or no. That's it and if I think you're lying, I cut. Each time you lie, I cut deeper, got it?"

She gasps, "Yes," as her tears pour onto the counter.

"Question one, was she a virgin when she slept with Hunter?"

The bitch whines like she doesn't want to answer so I press the blade a little harder. Not enough to cut yet but enough to let her know it's coming if she doesn't play by my rules.

She finally screams, "Yes!" so I nod and move on.

"Question two - Does Savy play sick and twisted games with men like you claimed?"

She's faster this time like she knows the jig is up. "Argg, no, no!"

I press her head harder into the counter. "Are you sure? You can elaborate on that."

"No! She's a loser. No man would even talk to her or look at her until you guys! The only reason Hunter fucked her was because his frat has a sex bingo contest and he picked her to fill his fuck-a-virgin square."

"Ah…fuck." I hear Tate swear softly when he finally gets how bad we fucked up by not believing in her.

"Question three - Why does Savy use her mother's maiden name instead of her dad's?"

The question has her spitting in annoyance. "Because she wants to be…normal! She doesn't want anyone to treat her like an heiress."

"Next question - Did you put strawberries in her drink that night to make her sick?"

The answer is quick and adamant. "NO! No, I didn't do it. I don't know how that happened!"

I want to cut this bitch so bad and see her blood wash all over my fingers but I actually do believe her so I lift the knife enough to yank her upright and then put it back against her throat.

"Last question - Why do you hate her so much?"

I'll give this cunt props for the anger and attitude that suffuses her face even with me holding a knife to her throat when she spits out, "Because she has EVERYTHING! She has the money, she has the fucking name I never got and she has the power that goes with it. She does NOTHING with it! It should be fucking mine! All of it should be mine."

I drop the knife away from her and nod at this pathetic excuse for a woman and toss the knife on the counter.

"I guess I do have one more question. Hmm, maybe a few more. Who pays for everything you have?" She makes a face telling me Savy does but refuses to answer so I keep going.

"Today's her twenty-first birthday, right? Does that mean she comes into her inheritance today?"

That gets me a petulant shrug making me chuckle darkly 'cause she just doesn't get how fucked she is. So, I spell it out.

"Final, final question. After what you just did to Savy, what do you think she's going to do to you now that she has full control over the purse strings?"

It takes her a beat but when she realizes the ramifications of what she's done to the wrong fucking person, she goes so red in the face that she almost turns burgundy. Her eyes are wide and filled with rage as they dart around the room like she's looking for a way to slam that genie back into the bottle and it makes me laugh darkly again.

I turn my back on her and wave at Beck, "Get that cunt out of my house."

ASHER

I pace back and forth through the kitchen as Beck hauls out the trash and Tate sits on the couch with his head in his hands. Jude grabs his phone and presses it to his ear mumbling, "Come on, doll, pick up." He punches the red button when she doesn't and goes to call her again. Fuck him. So she wasn't conning them but she sure as hell conned me and she lied about a hell of a lot more than that. Savy doesn't get a free fucking pass for any of that.

"Just let it go, Jude! She fucking played me and lied to all of us. Why are you still sniffing after her like a dog in heat?"

He bangs his cell against his forehead and roars through gritted teeth.

"Fuck you, Ash! You got your head so far up your own ass you can't see straight. Tell me… fucking tell me how she played you? Savy danced in a bar and you caught sight of her and became obsessed. She didn't make you that way. She didn't make you any promises, did she? No, she didn't say one goddamn word to you in two fucking years! You think because you watched her like that she owed you something?"

He tears at his hair and tries to call her again but doesn't get through so keeps ranting.

"You know why she danced in that cage, behind that mask? It's because she wanted to BE that woman but she was too afraid to be her in real life. She told me…" He barks out a crazed laugh. "She told me that you were the first man to SEE her, to look at her like she was something. She said you made her feel fucking…WORTHY! Argg! She was so fucking wrong. Savy's always been worthy. You're the one who isn't worthy of her."

He stabs a finger into my chest causing me to step back.

"When she met you here in real life, she was terrified of telling you because she knew you'd be furious that she wasn't the girl in the cage. She knew you would punish her for it. Why should she have told you when she didn't fucking trust you?"

I want to argue with him but he shoots me a dark look and asks, "Did you tell your Butterfly who you really are? Did you tell her where we come from? The shit we've done over the years? Didn't you owe her the truth? No? So why the fuck are you entitled to know her secrets, then?"

He turns away from me as his thumbs fly over the keyboard sending text after text and I go to the window and look out at the falling snow. I think back and remember the first time she came here. I answered the door and she almost had a seizure when she saw me. She could barely look at me after that until the night of the blizzard.

I remember now, I remember what a dick I was to her, telling her that we didn't need to deal with her being triggered by the storm. It was after that that she stopped being nervous around me and now I realize it was that moment that Savy threw up a wall to keep me out. She stopped caring, so my being a dick didn't phase her anymore.

My eyes crash closed as I remember that moment we had in the kitchen when I saw her tattoo for the first time. She said, fuck… she said it was supposed to remind her that she could be something, something she wasn't. It was supposed to mean that if she was brave enough, she could fly. And then she cried. I held her as she cried and I just thought it was PMS but she was trying to tell me her story in her own scared way. I took her up and put her to bed and she said how sorry she was and now I know that had nothing to do with being in my space. Savy was trying to tell me how sorry she was that she wasn't brave enough to tell me the truth.

Tate breaks me from my thoughts.

"That's how she got my dad to back off. It has to be. She used her name and probably some threats that the kind of name like Sevan could follow through on. She told him her real name to try and protect me. Even though she tries to hide it from the world. Why the fuck did she want it hidden? Why wouldn't she tell us?"

Beck shakes his head and then knocks it back against the wall he's leaning on.

"Didn't you hear that bitch? Savy just wanted to be normal. Think about the weight that that kind of name and fortune comes with. If people here knew, she would have been under a microscope constantly and they all would judge everything she did."

Tate throws his hands up in the air in frustration. "Fine! But why work two jobs? It's not like she needed the fucking money with billions in the bank. Fuck, she didn't need to stay here after her place blew up. She could have just bought a fucking building to move into!"

Jude throws his phone down in anger. "Are you that fucking stupid? She doesn't CARE about the money! She didn't care about our pro salary and bonus and she doesn't care about the billions her dad left her. She's got plastic Target dressers in her room for fuck sakes. All my doll cared about was having someone see her, care about her. She just wanted something real. And she...won't...answer...my...calls! FUCK!" He looks frantically between all of us. "One of you try, call her, text her!"

Tate shakes his head. "If Savy was going to answer for any of us, it would be you, Jude."

I turn away again not sure I want her to answer any of us. Just because Jude reasoned it out, doesn't mean I don't feel like I've been betrayed by her, lied to.

"Where is she? Where would she go? All her stuff's here," Jude mumbles as he tries her phone again.

After two years of only wanting one woman, I finally chose. I fucking picked Savy and it all fell apart. That reminds me of the charm bracelet of tiny books that I left on the table in the club so I scrub at my face, then throw him a lifeline.

"She was still wearing her Butter…her club clothes. She probably went back there."

His head jerks up from his phone and starts nodding quickly. "Yes! Okay, okay, Beck, I need you to drive me to the club!"

As one, we all start moving to the door but Jude throws an arm out blocking me from following. "No, not you. You don't get to go anywhere near my doll. You threw fuel all over my girl and lit the fucking match. You can stay right fucking here and burn for it."

"Jude…"

He cuts me off with a snarl. "Shut your hole! You're fucking done, Ash."

Tate and Beck look back at me with cautious expressions as they all gear up in jackets and then my three best friends, my family, leave me alone with the weight of what I've just done.

I stand there long after the front door slams closed trying to justify why all this is hers and not my fault but the longer I think about it the harder it gets. I finally move to the stairs and climb them, stopping at her open door. I take in the blue bed the color of her eyes, piled high with pillows, and breathe deeply of her peaches and cream smell. I let my fingers clench around the door jam. She did this, she had no right to… An image of her sad, wet blue eyes slides into place as she gripped my wrist and said, "Ash…I'm sorry, I'm so sorry."

I see her in her cage dancing for me. How her eyes always met mine. Not the sensual, sexual looks but the times her eyes were full of something else, something nameless. The times when I was having a shit day and her eyes said, 'it's okay, I see you, I'm here for you.' The two women, the Butterfly and Savy merge into one and it makes me realize that Savy's given me way more than I've ever given her and she never asked for anything back. The only thing Savy ever took from me was my eyes watching her and I gave those to her willingly.

"Fuck!"

BECKETT

I drive my truck through the snow to Masks as Jude continues to pound away on his phone trying to reach her. I'm so pissed at myself right now. I knew what a cunt that sister of hers was but I still let her pour her poison all over what I have with Savy. When she said that Savy was playing us and then when Ash seemed to confirm it, I just accepted it. I didn't even give her the benefit of a doubt.

The first thought that went through my head was that of course she would betray me, quickly followed by the toxic thought that she was just like my mom. It makes me realize that I've never let myself get close to a woman because I assume they would leave me. I can't let myself go through that again. My mother chose death over me and I've never let any woman close enough to feel that kind of pain again. I guess I'm fucked up more than I thought I was and Savy just paid the price for it.

Everything Jude said was true. She didn't owe us anything. Savy has a right to her secrets just like anyone else. She never expected me to tell her anything, she just accepted me for who I am and then tried to help me when she saw how much I was struggling with my future. But at the first sign of conflict, I automatically thought the worst of her. Fuck, she deserves better than me, than us. We've been careless with her from the very start. Making her feel like she wasn't enough to be worth pursuing. Savy gave all of us a second chance after we fucked up the last time but the sick feeling in the pit of my stomach tells me that we probably won't get a third chance.

"Pull up at the doors. Fuck finding a parking spot," Jude tells me and a quick glance over at him shows me just how tightly wound he is.

If Savy doesn't forgive us, if we lose her, Jude's going to go off the rails. I've never seen him like this for anyone before, let alone a woman. As soon as I pull up and throw the truck in park, he's out of the door with Tate quickly on his heels. I wait one moment and decide, fuck it, I'll eat the ticket. I shut it down and jump out quickly catching up to the others who are being blocked by Marco, the massive front door bouncer.

I've got a good foot of height on him but he probably has an extra fifty pounds of muscle on me. I might be able to take him in my current frame of mind but I've seen this guy fight and it's fucking dirty.

"There's nothing I can do, man. Stella says ban them, we ban them," he's telling Jude who starts tearing at his hair again.

"Urgh! I just need to talk to Savy, Marco! She works here as the Butterfly." Jude begs, causing Marco to cross his huge arms over his chest and glower at him.

"I know who Savy is, you dick. I don't know what the fuck you guys did to her but she was a wreck when Stella took her out of here."

"She's not here? Do you know where they went?" Jude whips out his wallet and pulls out all the cash in it and holds it out to the bouncer. "Please, man! I need to find her. I need to fucking fix this!"

Marco plucks the wad of cash from Jude's fingers with a huff of laughter.

"Good fucking luck with that. I heard Stella tell the driver to take them to the airport. She's fucking gone, asshole. You're too late. Now fuck off."

Jude bellows and lunges for him but Tate and I get a hold of him and drag him back to the truck. We wrestle him inside of it and climb in. I'm so fucking mad at myself, so damn scared that we broke her to the point that we won't be able to fix this. I ignore Jude as he rants at me for not taking him to the airport as I drive us home. Marco's right, we're too late. When I pull into the driveway and shut the truck off, I finally turn to Jude in the back seat.

"There's nothing we can do right now. We're all getting on a plane tomorrow for the bowl game. We're just going to have to ride this out until she comes back after the holidays. Jude, you have to shut it off for now. You and Tate need to focus on the game. Your whole futures depend on how you play in the next game and then Nationals when you fucking win. We will fix this thing with Savy when she comes back to school. You know we will! Think about how upset she'll be then if she's the reason why you fucked your whole future up. Lock it down, the both of you. Pour everything you're feeling into the game and win. Win for her."

Tate scowls but nods his understanding so I turn back to Jude. His eyes are closed but when he opens them it's a scary motherfucker looking back at me as he gives a curt nod and then slams out of the truck. Tate and I share a concerned look but there's not a lot we can do until Savy comes back to school so we follow our brother into the house.

TATE

We pull up to the house fresh off the plane from winning our bowl game. I'd like to say we're on a high of celebration but all of it is tainted by everything that's unresolved with our girl. Jude hasn't stopped blowing up her phone since that night but all his messages are showing delivered and not read. Same with mine and Beck's. I don't know if Ash has even tried reaching out to her. There's a major rift between him and Jude right now over it all so Beck and I are just trying to stay out of the line of fire.

We go up the front walk and are met by stacks of Amazon boxes and bags blocking the door. I was expecting some deliveries but not this many.

"Fuck, how many books did I order?" I muse, worried that I may have put in duplicate orders by mistake. Jude shoots me a look.

"You ordered books? For Savy?" At my nod, he rolls his eyes. "Well, so did I. I ordered everything on her kindle in paperback to replace the ones she lost in the fire."

I smirk at that knowing those faerie porn books will be read by him just as much as by Savy.

"I ordered all her favorite literary classics. All her copies were filled with little colored flags where she highlighted stuff. I thought we could go through them together and make new ones."

We both turn to Beck and he just shrugs. "I ordered her a bunch of fleecy clothes with cartoons on them and smelly candles. You know how she likes to be comfy and warm."

Ash grunts in annoyance and reaches past the stacks to unlock the door and then shoves a bunch of boxes into the house to make a path. I shoot a quick look at Jude and see the dark look in his eyes as his childhood friend disappears inside.

"Come on, let's carry this stuff up to her room. We should go buy some bookshelves and set them up so when she comes home it'll be all ready for her. It'll be a nice surprise."

Jude hums his agreement and some of the darkness leaves his expression. The three of us grab an arm full of boxes each and trudge up the stairs but Jude stops dead in her doorway and makes a noise like someone just stabbed him in the guts. I push him further into the room and everything inside of me just sinks. It's all gone. She's all gone. The only thing left in the room is the bare mattress and right in the middle of it is a key attached to a pink plastic butterfly. I drop the boxes and turn to grab Jude by the shoulders. He looks fucking wrecked.

"It doesn't matter. It's just temporary. We'll get her back. When she comes back to school we'll find out where she's moved to and we'll get her back. This isn't over, Jude. We're not going to fucking give up."

He nods slowly, sets the boxes down, and leaves the room with a crushed expression. My eyes meet Beck's and it's there that I see all the doubts I'm feeling but won't voice. Fuck, this might actually be over.

JUDE

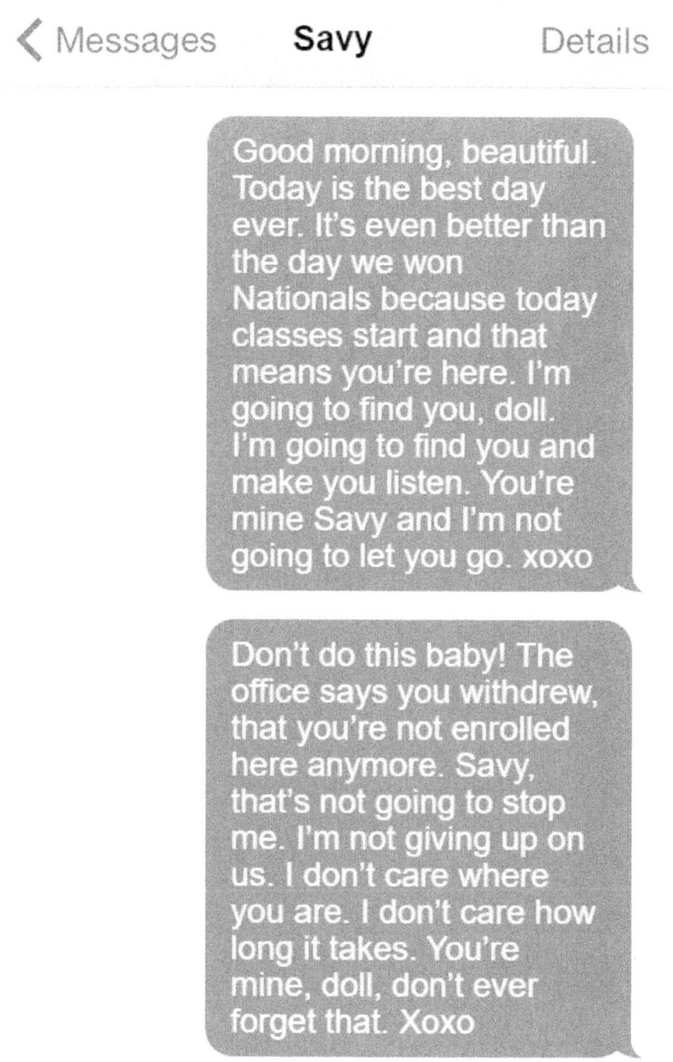
Messages
Savy
Details
Good morning, beautiful. Today is the best day ever. It's even better than the day we won Nationals because today classes start and that means you're here. I'm going to find you, doll. I'm going to find you and make you listen. You're mine Savy and I'm not going to let you go. xoxo
Don't do this baby! The office says you withdrew, that you're not enrolled here anymore. Savy, that's not going to stop me. I'm not giving up on us. I don't care where you are. I don't care how long it takes. You're mine, doll, don't ever forget that. Xoxo

2 months later

< Messages **Savy** Details

I wish you were here with me today. It's draft day. You're all I thought about when I got the call. All I wanted was to pull you into my arms and hold you. I promise you, baby, I'm not giving up. You're end game for me, doll. That's never going to change. Goodnight, angel. I hope you dream of me as I dream of you. Xoxo

BECKETT

Messages **Peaches** Details

I can't feel anything anymore. You're gone and now Jude and Tate are leaving too. Everyone always leaves. I just want to feel something again. I don't want to be alone.

I fumble the phone with alcohol-numbed fingers and cock my head to watch it fall to the floor before draining the last of the cheap whiskey from the bottle and then drop it too. It takes me a few minutes as my head spins to finally bend over to try to pick up my phone but I end up stumbling right into some chick that's passing by. She grabs a hold of me and pushes me back up against the wall to keep me upright with a laugh.

"Dude! You are so fucking wrecked. A big guy like you could flatten a girl like me. Are you a football player here?" She asks me with a little bit of a slur in her tone as she sways in front of me. I narrow my eyes a bit to see her through the whiskey haze and know right away she's not a sorority girl that I know. Her cheap clothes don't fit and she's got a large rose tattoo on full display between her large breasts spilling out of her low-cut top.

I swallow past the shitty taste in my mouth and say, "Football, yeah, was going to be a star. You don't go here?"

She leans against the wall beside me but ends up sliding right into me so I anchor an arm around her waist to keep us both up as she giggles.

"Nope, no college for me but some frat guy brought me here after my shift at the club was over." She runs a hand over my chest and her brows pop up at what she feels. "I was gonna fuck him for the free booze but he's scrawny compared to you. You wanna take a ride on me, big boy?"

My head drops back against the wall as the room tilts but I can feel her hands roaming over me and it feels good, better than what I've been feeling since my girl left so when she tugs on my arm, I let her lead me to a room and for a little while, even if it's meaningless, feel something.

When Jude finds me the next morning, I'm naked on some frat house bedroom floor with my wallet and phone stolen. All the numbness I was feeling shifts to guilt and self-loathing for being so fucking weak. It doesn't matter that she left me or that after two months I know she's not coming back. It still feels like I just cheated on Savy and I know more than ever now that she deserves better than me.

JUDE

I dump Beck into his bed and try hard not to slam the door as I leave. I'm pissed he fucked some random chick last night but the guy's a fucking disaster right now. It feels like everything has fallen apart since Savy left us. I scrub at my face as I head down the stairs ready to just get on a plane and haul her back here to fix all this shit.

"Is he okay?" Ash asks, causing me to send him a dark look.

"What do you think? No, he's not. The girl we love has ghosted us and he's about to lose the only family he's got."

I ignore the guilt that flashes across his face and turn to Tate instead.

"I can't fucking take this anymore, man. I need to go get her!"

Before Tate can answer me, Ash asks, "Where will she go?"

I check the snarl that I want to spit at him and instead just pin him with another dark look.

"Jude, I'm serious. You're going to go get her but then where will she go? The west coast with you or Florida with Tate? Or will she stay here with Beck and…me? You guys are out of here in a few months so if you bring her back, where will she go? Are you going to make her choose?"

Tate groans sadly. "Fuck. He's right, Jude. Even if you can convince her to come back, even if we can get her to forgive us, then what?"

My head turns from him to Ash and back before I snap and slam my fist through the closest wall with a roar of rage. God, everything hurts with her gone but knowing that they're right just hurts even fucking more. I have to let her go but I can't so I'll let her go…for now. Tate and I've got four years on our contracts but after three we can start working on negotiations. We both signed for more fucking zeros than I'll ever be able to spend in our lifetimes so for me, if I can't make a deal to get back to my doll, then fuck it, screw football. I'll just quit. I love football but it's never been what defines me, it's a fucking job. Football got me and Ash out of the ghetto and this contract will set me up for life. Having Savy and my brothers together as a family? That's worth more than anything catching a fucking ball could give me.

I turn back to them and shove my hair back from my face. "I'm not giving up on her. I will never give up on her…but…I'll wait. She's fucking worth it."

ASHER

The house is quiet as I chase beer after beer alone in the kitchen. I can't stop thinking about what Jude said. His certainty that Savy's worth it all. I've known that fucker since we were smashing windows of the abandoned textile factory on our way home from kindergarten and I never could have predicted that a woman could come between us. He barely tolerates me right now after what went down that night.

I can't believe she didn't come back. I always knew my Butterfly was one of a kind and this just proves it even more. Any other girl would have come back and made us suffer for what we did to her. There'd be drama and arguments and us groveling to try to get her back as a punishment but nope, not Savy. She just walked away and ghosted us completely and it's the worst fucking punishment I can think of.

I don't know why I was surprised by it. She always played her cards close to her chest and hid behind her masks and bars to keep people away. Her ghosting us like this after we hurt her is exactly what she would do and it's all my fault. Everything Jude ever said about me is true. I'm a fucking bastard. I fell in love with the Butterfly for so many reasons but the big one was that I didn't have to trust her. I could love her with bars between us so I didn't have to give pieces of myself to her that she could damage. It was simple and clean and I rode it for two years until Savy showed up.

Savy with her layers, with her sweetness, with her wet blue eyes that took me down. She stayed hidden because she didn't think that she was brave when the truth is, I'm the fucking coward. I was the one afraid. I kept saying I wanted more with the Butterfly but the truth was that I liked that she was at a distance, she was safe. Savy rocked all that and I fucking fell for her, picked her, but as soon as I was given an out by her cunt sister, I latched on to it and blew it up before it even started. Savy deserves so much more than that.

The place I come from and the people I grew up with are all fucked up. Poverty, crime, and neglect were just…life for us. It was ingrained in me from my first breath not to trust anyone, not even family, as they'd sell you out without a second thought. My sisters both ran as soon as they turned sixteen and found men to take care of them outside of the neighborhood. If it wasn't for Jude and football, I'd probably be in jail right now. It was him, Tate, and Beck that taught me to trust a little bit but I never extended that to anyone else. Seeing the way so many of the girls here tried different angles to hook my friends just reiterated that mistrust.

I drain the last of my beer and set the bottle next to the others as I reach down inside and dig deep. I want to be the man she deserves because she **is** worth it. So, I'll wait too but I'll spend the next years working on being the man Savy deserves and if I get another chance, I'll make it right. If she'll let me, I'll love that woman with everything I've got and it still won't be enough. I'll never be worthy of Savy but I'll spend every day fucking trying.

I flick the light off and walk up the stairs stopping at Jude's open door. He glances my way and it fucking kills me to see his expression harden when he sees it's me. I step into his room anyway and start the only way I know how.

"Brother…I'm so fucking sorry."

TATE

9 months later

Messages **Baby Girl** Details

Today should have been the best day of my life. I made it, baby girl. I played my first game as a pro athlete. I looked up into the crowd cheering for me and none of it meant as much as it should because you weren't there. I miss you, Savy. I'm so fucking sorry. Come back to me, baby.

BECKETT

1 year later

< Messages **Peaches** Details

Today I realized it's really over. I kept thinking we would find a way back to each other somehow. But I fucked up, peaches. I fucked up so bad. One moment of weakness from missing you, hating myself for what I let slip through my fingers and now no matter what, we will never be able to go back. You'll never forgive me and I don't blame you. You deserve so much more. You deserve everything. I love you, Savy. Please, find happiness.

JUDE

Messages **Savy** Details

Good morning, pretty girl! Can you believe it's been a year since I last kissed you? I saw you in the news yesterday. You looked so fucking beautiful I wanted to cry. I see you all the time on my screen but baby, it kills me that you never smile. I'm scared Sav, scared that I stole your smile. I'll give it back to you, I promise. I just need you to read my messages. I hope you have the best day. Xoxo

Excerpt from Page 6

Reclusive heiress and billionaire beauty, Savanna Sevan has sent shockwaves through the financial district today as she made her first power move since inheriting her father Stephan Sevan's billions and controlling interest in the Sevan Corporation. Her first girl boss move was to remove the entire board of directors and instate Mark Hanson as acting CEO. While Mr. Hanson has been in trust of the Sevan holdings since the death of Miss Sevan's father and until she came of age, he was limited by board approval. Many are holding their breath to see just what other plans Miss Sevan will have in the coming days.

JUDE

2 years later

< Messages **Savy** Details

2 fucking years, doll! 2 years and you haven't read any of my messages. Doesn't matter, I'm not going to stop. One day, I'll open this thread and your picture will be beside every message instead of that blue delivered check mark. I'm not giving up. I hope you have a great day and something happens to make you smile. I miss your smile, baby doll. Xoxo

Excerpt from Page 6

Billionaire beauty Savanna Sevan was spotted at the Gallagher Gala last night once again flying solo in her signature look. Her sleek, dark ponytail and black Versace gown were beautifully contrasted by her trademark red lipstick, and once again, no smile in sight. New York's most eligible bachelors will need to lay out all the stops to crack Miss Sevan's stoic countenance.

JUDE

3 years later

Excerpt from Page 6

Stoic billionaire beauty Savanna Sevan is still a mystery after three years on the scene. The elusive Miss Sevan is well known for her sharp business tactics at the helm of the Sevan Corporation but not much is known about her personal life as her privacy is fiercely guarded. The mysterious beauty has not been seen with an escort at any function to date and refuses all interviews on her private life. All of New York society is mesmerized by her and many an eligible bachelor has failed to crack her indifferent mask. There is a long line of eager gentlemen hoping to win the first smile from her.

JUDE

4 years later

< Messages **Savy** Details

Good morning, angel. You looked amazing in that dress but I liked you better in the blue one. I know black is your signature color now but I remember how good you looked in nothing but pink. Soon, doll, soon. The plan worked. We'll be seeing you really fucking soon. I hope you're ready. Xoxo

JUDE

4 years and 5 months later

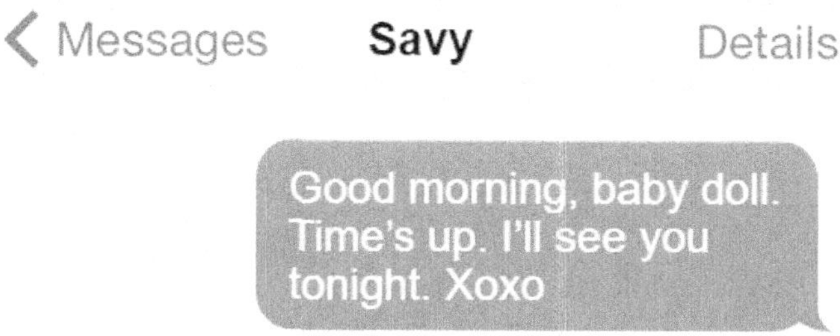

Excerpt from Page 6

All of New York society is grasping for tickets to tonight's VIP Grand Opening of the city's newest hot spot, Masks. Socialites, celebrities, and sports stars are stacked up on the gold-plated guest list. Rumor has it a certain unsmiling billionaire beauty has partnered with club owner Stella Banks in the venture. Curious minds want to know if Miss Sevan will be wearing a new mask at the event or sticking with the one she wears daily.

JUDE

I stare at my phone, see the blue check mark that my daily text to her has been delivered and give it a few minutes but as usual, it isn't read. I smirk and toss the phone onto the counter and turn to the others. Ash meets my gaze cautiously. We're still not back to where we were before he fucked us all over but if tonight goes well, I might finally be able to forgive him completely.

Beck drains the last of his coffee and sets his cup on the counter with a sigh.

"Still nothing?" He asks and I shake my head causing him to sigh again. "I mean, we're in the play now but are you sure, Jude? It's a lot of faith to go on after over four years without her reading a single one of your messages. All the letters and gifts we sent over the years? She might have moved on, man."

I cross my arms and smirk. "The last time I let my faith in her slip, we lost her. I'm not giving up now. Yes, she hasn't read my messages or responded to anything we sent but think about that. Every day for over four years, a notification pops up on her phone and she has to swipe it away. She's done that over fifteen hundred times. Why? Why not just block me? Why not change her number? No, every day Savy sees my name on her phone. She hasn't moved on. Besides, she's been in the media almost as much as we have since she went to work at Sevan. They follow and fawn over her because she doesn't date, she doesn't smile and she's a complete mystery. We'd know if she had moved on. Tonight's the night. It's the first step in getting her back."

Beck rubs at his mouth, looks to Tate and Ash who both nod, and then pulls out a slim folder from inside his suit jacket and tosses it down on the counter.

"Alright, here are the tickets. The car will pick us up here at nine. Make sure you all have your masks."

We hear the front door open and a high-pitched laugh causes Beck to turn in that direction with a resigned look. When he looks my way again, he nods one more time.

"Good luck. I hope you get your girl back."

"**Our** girl, Beck. We are getting **our** girl back." I tell him with conviction but he only shoots me a tight smile and then heads to the front of the house.

Doubt floods in briefly but I push it away. I know my girl, even after four years. She can't have changed that much. Her sweet heart will open for him, for us all. We just need to pry it open a crack to get back in.

SAVY

My thumb hovers over the text preview window notification on my phone.

Good morning, baby doll…

It's a sick, twisted addiction I allow myself. I get to see his first words to me and then like every day, swipe the message away unread. I should have blocked his number years ago instead of torturing myself like this but I can't seem to let go and apparently, neither can Jude.

I sigh, drop my phone back into my bag and tilt my head back to take in the six open levels above me in Stella's new club. I stay out of the way of the busy staff moving every which way as they stock bars and straighten tables preparing for tonight's opening. My gaze goes to all the hanging cages that masked dancers will be performing in as memories of hard, jade-green eyes wash over me.

"Sure you don't want to strap on your wings for old time's sake, babes?"

I arch a brow at my best friend and shake my head.

"I can just see how that would play out in the press. No, thank you."

Stella runs a hand through her sharply angled blond bob as her eyes dart from place to place with nerves.

"Don't," I tell her. "Stop with the doubts, Stell. I never would have invested in this if I didn't believe it would be a major success." She hums half in agreement before stopping a passing person to check on the stemware racks he's carrying.

Stella moved to New York last year when the owner of the club we used to work in closed it down to retire to Florida. It's been good to have her here near me as she pushes me out of the tight little box I've lived in since leaving school. She was working as an assistant manager in one of the popular city nightclubs but was frustrated that none of her suggestions were ever considered to make the club better. Too much wine one night had me telling her I would bankroll a new club and that she should use the same concept and name of the club we first met at. I knew it would translate well from a college town to the city and after careful research, Masks 2.0 was born.

"Gawd, I'm going to lose my mind before the doors even open! You need to distract me, Sav. What's happening with you? Do you have your dress for tonight?"

I arch my brow at her and nod slowly considering she's the one who picked it out. Stella approves almost all of my outfits to keep the dreaded corduroy from making a resurgence in my wardrobe. She sighs and tugs on her hair again while hitting me with a cautious look.

"I haven't wanted to bring it up but…did you see the news?"

My shoulders tense and I let my indifferent mask settle across my features causing her to huff.

"Stop it! You know you don't get to wear the Sevan heiress mask with me."

I roll my eyes and look away. "Of course, I saw it. How could I not? It's been posted everywhere for the last few weeks."

"Are you nervous? With both of them being traded to play for the Kings, there's a chance you will run into at least one of them."

I cross my arms over my satin-breasted, tailored black suit jacket and lift my chin. "Highly doubtful.

It's not like we will be running in the same social circles."

Stella bites her lip and moves closer, lowering her voice. "Maybe it wouldn't be so bad if you did, though. It could give you some closure. Let you finally move on?" I drop my eyes from her knowing look. "Babes, it's been over four years. You need to try to have a life besides work. You're young, rich, and beautiful. You should be dating and living life to the fullest!"

"I have moved on and I don't want to date. I'm perfectly content with the male in my life, thank you very much."

She smirks at that but then places a hand on my arm. "Is he still sending you texts every day?"

I shrug one shoulder but nod.

"Savy, did it ever occur to you that maybe they were traded here to be closer to you?"

My mouth goes dry making it hard to swallow but I still shake my head. "Don't be ridiculous. As you said, it's been over four years. I was just some stupid girl they messed around with in college that they think screwed them over. I don't know why Jude still texts me but I haven't read a single one of them so it's not like he'd think there was anything there." I push away from the wall with a frown. "It doesn't matter anyway. Even if for some deranged reason they're here for me, that's not going to happen. I'll never let anyone hurt me the way they did again. I need to go. I have back-to-back meetings today. I'll see you tonight, Stell. I promise it's going to be a smash hit. You have nothing to worry about."

I quickly squeeze her arm and I stride from the club out to where my driver is waiting for me at the curb. I settle back into the cool leather seats, slide on my favorite oversized black sunglasses and smooth my sleek ponytail as he makes his way through traffic to my building. It takes considerable effort not to let myself think about Jude Dixon and Tate Valor being in the same city as me for the first time in four years. Even as I pull out my phone and start replying to emails, there's a small red light flashing in the back of my mind that Stella might be right, that they might be here for me.

Hours later, I rub at the growing ache between my eyes as I flip the folder closed in frustration. I specifically told Mark that we wouldn't be moving in this direction. He's been an excellent CEO for the last four years as I've cut my teeth on every aspect of the company but I still have final approval on major decisions. The direction he wants us to go doesn't fit the new image and branding I've been pushing us toward over the last two years but even after telling him that, he's moved ahead. A glance at the time has me sighing and reaching for the intercom.

"Mandy, can you bring my lunch in and see if Mark has any time in his schedule for a meeting this afternoon, please?"

"Right away, Miss Sevan," comes back to me through the speaker.

I reach for another file and start scanning the documents inside. Some time later a strangled sound has my head popping up.

"Guh! I would pay to be the meat in that man sandwich!"

My brows pop up at such a strange, out-of-place thing for my assistant to say. She huffs out a laugh and rushes to place my lunch on the corner of my desk.

"Sorry! I just wasn't expected to be greeted by ***that*** when I walked in here."

"Excuse me? Greeted by what?"

She laughs again and points behind me so I spin my chair and choke back a gasp.

My office has floor-to-ceiling windows giving me a perfect view of the tower across from mine. Often, advertisers will pay to have images wrapped onto one entire side of buildings for huge displays. What I'm looking at right now straight across from me is a building-size image of the two newest players for the New York Kings, Jude Dixon, and Tate Valor. My heart rate goes through the roof as I stare at the two men who once meant so much to me. It's not like I haven't seen them over the last four years. Google is a blessing and a curse when it comes to looking up an ex…whatever they were to me.

They look the same but different. They're older and a little bit harder looking. Jude's wild mane of messy hair is shorter and tighter but still white blond and I can see some new ink creeping up his neck under the jersey he's wearing. Tate still looks like the football god he is. His dark blond hair and square jaw give him that all-American look as he clutches a football. I sigh and slowly spin my chair back around putting my back to them.

"Mandy, I need you to track down the management of that building. Tell them I'll pay to have that image removed and put on the other side of the building. That's not something I can look at every day."

My assistant's brows pop up in surprise but she quickly nods and I'm grateful that she doesn't ask any other questions.

"Mr. Hanson's unavailable today. He's left for the weekend to go out of town. Do you want me to book you in with him for Monday?"

I groan in frustration but nod and dismiss her. I quickly fire off an email to Mark letting him know we need to talk on Monday and then glance at the lunch sitting on the corner of my desk but leave it there. It's hard to have an appetite when you can feel two sets of eyes staring at the back of your head. I try to ignore all thoughts of them and reach for another file. It's going to be a really long day.

By the time I make it home, I have less than an hour to get ready for Stella's opening. My driver, Patrick, follows me up the steps to the brownstone carrying the garment bag that contains my dress and a few other bags. He waits behind me as I unlock the door and punch in the alarm code before stepping in behind me. A deep menacing growl greets him but he's used to Mo's reaction after two years so he stands his ground as my baby boy snarls and bares his teeth at him.

"That's enough, Mo!" I tease the big lug. He steps back and plops his beautiful Kardashian-sized rump to the marble floor, his tongue hanging out and delirious love swimming in his big brown eyes for me. I drop my bag and reach to take everything from Patrick.

"I'll be out in an hour if you want to go grab some food. Make sure you charge it on the company account."

He nods my way and winks at Mo who lifts one side of his mouth to show his fangs and steps back out. As soon as the door closes behind him, I let my mask slip away and smile for the first time in hours as I drop to my knees and bury my face in Mo's long shaggy brown and white fur.

"There's my big boy! Who's a good boy? Did you go out with Sara for a big walk? Did you chase all the squirrels and terrorize all the men of the city? Yes you did, didn't you? My big ferocious sweetie!"

I let the stress of the day roll off of me as I rub and coo to him while he butts me back onto my bottom with a love attack. This right here is all the male I need in my life. I laugh as he swipes my neck with his oversized tongue and remember how resistant I was when Stella dropped him off two years ago. He's a mixed breed with some St. Bernard and Maremma thrown in and he's perfect in every way. Even though I now have to buy lint rollers in bulk, I wouldn't give him up for the world. Stella was in town for a visit at the time and hated how I lived in this big house all alone so she surprised me with Mo when I came home from work one night and she was right. Having him to come home to eased the ache inside of me that I've suffered with for the last 4 years. The fact that Mo hates all men was just an added perk that amuses me constantly.

I push to my feet and gather up everything I dropped to greet him and head deeper into the huge house to the back door to let him out. While he does his business, I fill his food dish and water and snag a quick frozen meal for myself. We eat together while I tell him all about my day and apologize for leaving him alone again to go out tonight. I very rarely spend my evenings anywhere but here with him draped over my lap but Stella's opening is not something I can miss. Mo bounds up the stairs ahead of me to the third level where my bedroom is and dive-bombs my bed to roll around and mess up the covers while I strip down and hit the shower.

Getting ready is fast for me with not having to do anything but run a hot straightener through my hair to keep my ponytail sleek. I darken my makeup to match the dress I'm wearing and blink a few times at my reflection with a frown. It's been over three years since I got laser eye surgery and I still feel vulnerable without my large glasses to hide behind. With a sigh, I slick on my red matte lipstick that will last all night and go remove the dress from its garment bag. I hold it up and take a deep breath. It's shorter and more shape fitting than I prefer but for a nightclub opening it checks all the boxes. It's black metallic mesh over a bodycon slip that hugs all my curves. The front dips down low showing the swell of my breasts and body tape holds it in place so nothing will slip out while I dance. The front and back form a point between my thighs with the sides cut up higher. The back dips down to the small of my back and has inch-wide straps crossing in the middle of my back.

I add extra tape to the sides to keep the dress in place and not show the tattoos on my right side that have grown from the single small butterfly I used to only have on my hip. Those are not for the public to see, those are mine.

I slide into the strappy silver stilettos and buckle them up before jumping up and down a few times in front of the mirror to make sure everything stays in place. I tilt my head to the side to study the look with the matching mask in hand and huff out a small laugh that all I need is to add wings and I could rewind time to four years ago. Except, I no longer need a fabric mask to hide behind to look like this.

The one I crafted for my public expression does the job of keeping everyone at arm's length now.

I fill the silver clutch with everything I need and text Sara to remind her to swing by and let Mo out in a few hours and then slide my cell into the purse, ready to go. I can already feel my anxiety ramping up so I stop in the kitchen on my way to the door and toss back two shots of Patron-branded courage. I may not hide as much as I used to but courage is still sometimes hard to dredge up for me. I swing a black satin wrap over my arm, stop at the hall mirror to fix the mask in place, and step out of my house. Patrick is waiting out front and swings open the back door to the SUV for me offering his hand to help me up into it.

SAVY

Cameras flash nonstop as I step out in front of the club onto the red carpet. I stand and pose with a hand on my hip and a blank, indifferent expression as they get their fill, ignoring all questions tossed my way. I just keep Stella's words front and center as I push down the nerves and anxiety this still brings me. I was terrified the first time I had to go to an event after I accepted my inheritance.

"Babes, please! You spent over two years shaking your barely covered ass in front of way worse crowds. This is when you bring the Butterfly back. You strut across that carpet wearing her mask with your eyes snapping a great big fuck you to all those cameras. Savy, they can't touch the Butterfly so be her when you need to be."

When I've had enough, I stride into the new and improved Masks and Stella greets me at the door with a nervous smile. We brush our cheeks together as she takes my hand and leads me deeper into the already dancing crowd. The music's pounding, the lights are flashing and the Patron starts loosening me up. She leans close so I'll hear her over the noise.

"I've got your table on the fourth level VIP but I seriously need to dance some of these nerves off. You up for that?"

I arch a brow at her, keeping my public mask in place as there are photographers scattered throughout the club, and tug her to the middle of the dance floor. She snags my purse and wrap, hands it off to a waitress to take up to my table, and then we start to move and it feels so damn good. It's been forever since I danced in public and I forgot how happy it makes me to get lost in the beat and lights. Stella gets called away after only a few songs but I'm in it now so I wave her off and keep dancing alone as other dancers move closer and then away.

I'm lost in it with my hands above my head and my hips swaying when another dancer moves up behind me. I grind into it even as a large warm hand slides across my stomach to anchor me against him. I want to smirk at how good it feels to have a hot body pressed against my back but I've trained myself to not react in any way so I just lean back and rest my head against a hard chest. I take a deep breath and bite my red-painted lip as heat fills my core at the hardness I can feel against my back. It's been so fucking long since a man had his hands on my body that I almost forgot how good it could feel.

Whoever I'm dancing with matches me move for move but when his hand slides up between my breasts to caress my neck I try to pull away. I don't do this in public…ever. I turn my head to tell him to let go and catch the smell of citrus and something else that I would know anywhere. It's a unique scent that I'll never forget. It's all Jude. My body comes to a stop as I freeze in place, unable to say the words, unable to say anything. He knows the second it clicks for me because he chuckles next to my ear.

"You still have all the moves, baby doll."

It's a fight to keep my face expressionless as I try to pull away. His fingers tighten around my throat possessively and hold me closer.

"Nowhere to run to now, doll. I'm done chasing."

I suck in a breath and grind out, "Let…me…go."

His fingers slide up to my chin and he tilts my head up and back so I'm forced to look at him. Our mouths are a breath away from each other and his golden eyes are filled with so much emotion that the Tequila churns in my stomach and my heart does an extra beat.

"Never. I told you the last time I was deep inside of you that you're mine and I fucking meant it."

My brows crash down and I give the slightest shake of my head, denying it. I force a hardness into my tone when I reply.

"You burned any chance of that to ash. Let me go, Jude, now."

Amusement dances in his eyes as his fingers slide back down my throat in a caress that has goosebumps raising all over my skin.

"We're not done, baby doll. I'll let you go for now but get ready 'cause I'm coming for you."

He drops his arm from around me and I stagger a few steps away trying with everything I have to keep a blank face and not look back at him. I slide between other dancers as my heart races. I get bumped in a different direction and almost lose my balance on my towering heels but strong arms wrap around me and pull me up against another hard chest. I blink my eyes a few times to clear the daze of seeing Jude again and look up straight into desire-filled jade green eyes. I suck back a quick gasp and my head spins.

"Hello, Butterfly. It's so fucking good to watch you dance again."

I try to rear back but another body slides up behind me and rough hands grasp my hips.

"Baby girl, you still take my breath away." Is murmured directly into my ear. I start to shake and have a hard time pulling in air. Why are they here? What do they want from me? Is this some twisted revenge thing because they thought I was playing them due to Vanessa's lies?

A broken, "S-stop!" rasps out of me and their arms fall away letting me step to the side and bolt for the stairs. I need space, I need a minute to…the last of them steps in front of me blocking my way to the stairs and I force my head back to look up into his icy blue eyes as a sob tries to break free.

"Peaches, please, just give us a chance to explain."

I jerk my head so hard in denial that my ponytail whips around and brushes my face and then I'm darting around him and pounding up the stairs while clutching the banister as my feet wobble in my heels. I can't DO this! Not here, not in public. There are too many eyes on me. Too many cameras and gossips. I refuse to let them steal my mask and expose me so publicly.

When I get to my table, instead of reaching for my purse and running, my shaky hand goes to the glass tray of shot glasses that the bottle service has poured out and left. I toss back two of them back to back in the hopes that the alcohol will numb some of the raging emotions crashing through me. When a hand lands on my shoulder I flinch so hard to the side that I almost go down. Thankfully, Stella grabs my elbow to steady me.

"Whoa! Are you sure you should be drinking like that, babes? There's a lot of press still here."

I stare at her wordlessly and she reads the distress in my eyes because her smile slips away and she moves closer to me with a look of concern.

"What? What happened?"

I manage to choke out, "T-they're…here."

Understanding washes over her face and she jerks her head around to look but her hand tightens on my elbow and her body goes tense next to me.

"I banned you from the last club. Don't think I won't do it again at this one no matter how fucking special you are now," she growls out harshly.

I move my head slowly and take in the four men that have followed me up the stairs. They're all wearing masks just like the rest of the clubgoers but that doesn't stop me from feeling the full weight of all four sets of eyes.

"Easy, we just want to talk to her. We're not looking to make trouble." Tate says with a hand held out toward me.

Stella laughs harshly. "I don't think Savy gives a fuck what you want." She turns to me and asks, "Savy, you got any fucks to give?"

I meet each one of their gazes and see emotions that shouldn't be there after the way we left things. I don't understand why they are here, why they want to talk to me after all this time so I slowly start shaking my head and say, "Go fish."

The corner of Jude's lips twitches up and he crosses the few steps between us until his scent fills my nose and then he sinks onto one knee, making my whole body jolt back. His warm hands wrap around one of my ankles and his face is directly in front of the juncture of my legs that starts to pulse at having his hands on my body again.

"Your strap came loose. Can't have my doll falling and messing up all her perfection."

He rises to his feet and lifts my hand to his mouth as his lips brush over my knuckles and then takes a half step back. The breath I didn't know I was holding gushes out of me. His eyes burn into me as he tilts his head to the side.

"Enjoy your night, baby doll. I'll be seeing you real soon."

With one more smirk, he turns away and the three others peel off one by one to follow him. I'm frozen in place as my eyes track their progress down the stairs, level by level, and then out to the front lobby where they disappear.

Stella's hand slips into mine and squeezes.

"Oh, babes. You're so fucked."

SAVY

"You been playing me, doll?"

That one sentence haunts my dreams over and over during the little amount of sleep I manage to get. Mo flops over my legs and pins them to the bed like he's trying to get me to stay still from all the tossing and turning I've done. I give up just as dawn starts to creep in and reach for the remote, flicking through channels to try to find something to take my mind off of the four men that have re-entered my life. A strangled groan escapes me when both Jude and Tate flash on the screen of ESPN as I'm clicking past. As much as I want to click on the next channel, I can't bring myself to. While the sportscasters debate what the trades will do for the NY Kings next season my mind goes back to the months after I left them.

> *"You sure you want to watch this, babes?" Stella asks me.*
>
> *I peek an eye out from under the plush snuggly Jude bought for me and try to blink away the ache of swollen itchiness from so much crying. It's been almost*

three weeks since that night and the pain still thrums through me even though I promised myself in that cold parking garage I would burn it, them, all out from my mind and heart. I turn my eyes to the TV and watch the clock run down in the final quarter of the national championship game. All the players race out onto the field at the win and hoist Tate and then Jude up on their shoulders. They've both played an amazing game. The cameras focused on them often showing me the intensity in their eyes and their grim expressions. Even after points were scored, they chest bumped and high fived but they never smiled and I know it's because they are furious with me and what they believed I did.

They both get pulled over to the press and all the standard questions are asked and canned answers given until the pretty blond reporter asks, "You both seemed incredibly focused and especially fierce out there today. What was the driving force for you that brought home the win?"

Jude's eyes slide away from her to stare into the camera and he tips his head up with a hard expression. "We won it for our girl and we wish she was here to see it."

I suck in a shocked sob and dive for the remote to shut the TV off as tears well up again.

"What did that mean?" Stella practically screams but I just shake my head.

"It didn't mean anything. They…don't mean anything."

She drops down beside me on the couch with a sigh. "Sav, maybe you should read the messages they sent? Maybe it was all a misunderstanding. They just said on national television that…"

"No! They can say whatever they want. It's too late, I saw the look in their eyes. I heard the hateful words that Ash screamed at me and was gutted by Jude's lack of faith in me. It's over! It's all over!"

She slings an arm around my shoulder and squeezes. "Alright, babes, then let's get you off this couch and make a plan for your future."

I sniff back my tears and sigh. "God, Stella, I'm such a mess."

She brushes the hair away from my face and nods. "Yes, you are. But, caterpillars have to dissolve into a disgusting pile of goo before they become butterflies." She waves a finger up and down me. "So, you know, just keep going and we'll find your wings eventually."

I snort out a laugh and let her pull me from the couch.

And we did. It took a while but I did find my wings with her help. I knew I needed a change. I couldn't go back to being that weak little bookworm as Ash called me. I wasn't going back to school to attend classes. I was going to finish out my degrees remotely and start shadowing Mark at the office to learn everything I could about the massive Sevan Corporation I had inherited. That meant I'd be out in the public eye so Stella helped me put together a wardrobe of designer brands for the first time in my life. Almost everything I agreed to ended up being black. She argued against it but the color fit my mental state so she turned it into a signature style that I still wear to this day. The bun I always wore turned into a sleek ponytail and I agreed to get laser eye surgery when she insisted that I would need to wear contacts every day to fit the style.

I didn't plan to never smile. I was just in such a dark place for the first year after I left school and the press picked up on it and ran with it so I added it to the public mask I wear and save all my smiles for Mo and Stella in private. The whole image works for me as it keeps almost everyone at a distance. Stella tells me that most people and guys are intimidated by it which I think is hilarious. No one has ever been intimidated by me…ever. I was always the one afraid of others but again, it works to keep most people away. After what happened with the guys, I don't want anything to do with men, period. I let down my walls and started opening my heart to them and they broke me. No one will ever get the chance to do that to me again.

Sick of my depressive thoughts, I snap off the TV and toss the remote to the side, throw back the covers and roll out of bed. I snag a faded orange zip-up hoodie to wear over my sleepwear and grab my phone. My fingers squeeze around it briefly as I frown at it, biting my lip. I shake my head and nudge the stupid thing awake and breathe a sigh of…disappointment…relief? There's no notification from Jude. I rub at the ache between my eyes. Did he finally listen? Has he given up? Does that make me…happy?

I rumble out a small groan of frustration at my ridiculousness and slip the phone into my pocket and then follow Mo down the stairs to the back door. I shut the alarm off and crack the door for him to race out with a growling bark as he chases whatever birds are out there and then go to the front door to collect my morning newspapers. I start the coffee pot and while it brews I flip through the first paper and choke out a curse when I see a picture from last night.

Someone must have snapped it as Jude kneeled at my feet to fix my stiletto strap. The look on his face is almost as bad as the one on my own and the press made full use of it with the caption, '*Football phenom, Jude Dixon cracks the gates to Billionaire Beauty, Savanna Sevan with a…*'

I don't bother reading the rest but I do take a minute more to study our expressions. Jude's looking up at me with what could only be described as an adoring look and I'm looking down at him with my mouth open in surprise but it's the look of pure longing covering my face that makes me toss the section of paper into the garbage. Damn him for showing up and making me feel that! Damn them all for pulling my mask off in public.

I snatch a mug from the cupboard and slam it to the counter before splashing hot coffee on my hand when I jerk the pot over it and hiss out another curse. I force myself to take a few deep breaths, shove my hair back away from my face and carry the cup to the back door to try to enjoy one of my few mornings of freedom. I have an oasis set up in my backyard with comfortable seating surrounded by pots of thick flowers. Sundays are the only day I force myself not to work. I sit outside, play with Mo, and occasionally let myself read a book. My reading choices are something else that has changed dramatically in the last four years, too. I stick to the classics or nonfiction. I haven't cracked a romance novel in four years. I don't believe in it anymore so I refuse to read about it. There's a stack of those types of books unread in my library that Jude has sent me over the years. He might still believe in romance but I sure as hell don't so they'll stay unread.

I nudge the back door open with my hip as I go out sideways, coffee in one hand, the rest of the newspaper in the other.

"Mo! Are you ready to…"

My cup crashes to the flagstone dumping all the coffee out but thankfully doesn't shatter as it slides to the table where an unexpected visitor sits with a smirk.

"Morning, baby doll."

I sputter out nonsense as my glaring eyes track down to the big head cuddling in his lap. Mo's eyes are rolled back in his head and his tongue hangs out the side in ecstasy as Jude's tatted fingers dig into the fur between his ears and rub.

"You traitor!" I huff out, causing Mo to roll one eye my way with a groan but he makes no move to free himself from under Jude's ministrations. So much for my fur baby hating all men.

"Sorry about the coffee, doll, but I brought you one so, fair trade?"

I glare at him as I skirt around the mess of coffee and step toward him.

"What are you doing here? How did you get in?" I practically growl at him.

He just shrugs one muscular shoulder and nudges the takeout coffee in my direction.

"It wasn't all that hard to climb over your back wall and I'm here because you won't read my messages so I decided to say good morning in person so you can't ignore me anymore."

His smirk softens and I catch the hint of vulnerability that crosses through his eyes when he says softly, "Good morning, beautiful."

My teeth bite down on my bottom lip to stop myself from softening toward him and instead spin away to go back into the house. I hear the seat he's in scrape back and then his hand is on my arm and he's gently pulling me back around.

"Baby, stop, please? It's been over four years, Savy. Please, talk to me."

There's so much emotion packed into his tone and in his golden eyes that my stomach does a slow flip and my heart squeezes painfully even as I'm shaking my head.

"Why? Why, Jude? Like you said, it's been over four years! There's nothing to talk about." I yank my arm from his and throw a hand through my hair realizing that I didn't put it up this morning. My other hand comes up to gather it but Jude steps into me and lightly grasps my wrists, stopping me.

"Leave it, doll. You don't need to hide from me, you never did."

I choke out, "S-stop. Stop all of this! There's nothing here for you, for any of you. It was just a few months of fun years ago and you all made your choice to end it when you believed Vanessa's shit. Why can't you let it go, Jude?"

He uses my wrists to yank me closer so my chest hits his. "The same damn reason you can't let it go, doll. I fucking love you. That never changed!"

I try to pull away but he growls and slides his hands around me to hold me still so I shake my head in denial and lie to him, lie to myself.

"I did let it go. I let all of you go when I got on that plane and never came back. I built a new life here and it has no room for any of you in it."

A small smile pulls at his lips as his fingers press into my lower back.

"I might have believed you, doll, but you're wearing my fucking shirt."

I jerk my chin down to stare at the soft, faded t-shirt I sleep in under the open hoodie and try to come up with a reason for him why I would sleep in his clothes after all these years but come up blank. He chuckles and starts to rub my back causing a tremor to run through me.

"That's Tate's hoodie too, isn't it? You haven't let it go, baby doll. None of us have. You might not read my messages but every morning you see my name and you never blocked me, never changed your number. Savy, none of us are ever going to let it go. We belong with each other. Read all the messages, Savy. Catch up to the rest of us."

I swallow past the tears that are starting to clog my throat.

"Let me go, Jude."

He stares into my eyes and then slowly starts to nod. "Yeah, I'll let you go today but I'm going to keep climbing whatever walls you put between us, baby. I'm done waiting so get your head straight. This is happening."

He leans into me and brushes his lips over my forehead and then drops his arms and steps back from me. He grabs the take-out coffee and presses it into my hands.

"Sorry about the coffee. Read the messages, Savy."

I stand there speechless as he turns and strides toward my back wall, pausing long enough to give Mo another scratch on the head. He reaches up and pulls his body straight up and over the brick wall in one powerful move. I stand there until Mo comes and butts his head against my hip. Sinking to the ground, I wrap an arm around his thick neck and bury my face in his fur.

Jude Dixon just told me he loves me and I have no idea what to do about it.

SAVY

I spent the rest of the day in bed with the sheets thrown over my head trying to pretend that never happened. My mind won't stop, though. It takes me back to analyze every moment the five of us spent together. Every conversation, every touch, rolls through my messed-up head over and over again but it always ends the same way. That horrible day, that fucking night when everything crashed down and they didn't choose me, didn't choose us. I pick up my phone, swipe open the messaging app where all their unread messages wait and just stare at it for a minute before throwing the damn phone across the room.

I force myself to remember the pain of that night and all the nights that came after. I can't DO that again. I barely made it through the first time. No, I made my choice. No men, no romance, no pain. I have a course set for my future. I'm going to keep working toward building on what my dad started with the Sevan Corporation. There's no room for anything else.

I'm exhausted by the time I walk onto my floor Monday morning but my decision is made and my mask is firmly back in place. I walk past my assistant's empty desk, surprised as she usually makes it in before me, and push through to my corner office and immediately feel my blood pressure skyrocket.

"What are you doing in my office?"

I growl at Tate whose face is filled with a charming smile for Mandy. She's blushing at him with an adoring look but turns my way with a smile.

"Oh! This is Tatum Valor. He's the…"

I cut her off with a glare. "I know who he is, Mandy. What I asked is, what is he doing in my office?" I snap, causing both her and Tate to frown.

"I…he…um…" She stutters out but Tate steps toward me.

"Don't be mad at her, Savy. I kind of bullied my way in. I was hoping to take you to lunch later."

I squeeze my fingers tight around the handle of my briefcase and bite back the million curses I want to let loose. I stride past both of them and drop my case on my desk, putting it between us and then pin my assistant with a hard look even as her wide eyes shoot back and forth between Tate and me.

"Mandy! Being a minor celebrity doesn't give anyone a free pass into my office. Please, remember that in the future."

Her gaze goes back and forth a few more times and then she blurts out excitedly, "You two ***know*** each other?"

I shake my head in exasperation at the star-struck look in her eyes even as Tate chuckles.

"Now would be a good time for you to leave. Be sure to review the nondisclosure agreement you signed when you were hired."

I tell her with a hard enough tone to have her flinching and dashing for the door. I roll my head on my neck already feeling the tension in it and my shoulders. Eight in the morning and I already wish the day was over.

I turn my eyes to Tate but don't speak, just take in the changes from the last time I saw him this close in the light of day. He's filled out…everywhere. If anything, his jaw is even more square but now it's covered with a close-cropped blond beard that does nothing to hide the dimples he flashes my way when he smiles. He's wearing a dark, navy blue dress shirt that stretches across his wide chest. It's open at the collar and his sleeves are rolled up, exposing his muscular forearms. Dark grey dress pants cling to his thick thighs and seeing him so close again has me pushing hard to keep my mask in place.

"What do you want, Tate?"

There is no pre-amble, no attempt at small talk, and no hesitation when he answers. "You."

I huff out a humorless laugh and turn my back on him to look out the window but then groan when he and Jude stare back at me from the building across the way. I hear him laugh softly and then feel his heat against my back. He doesn't touch me but he's close enough that only an inch separates us.

"Baby, I missed you so fucking much. It's so good to see you." He breathes next to my ear.

My core clenches causing my fingers to make a fist. I hate that he still has the ability to make my body react to him. I force that thought down and skirt away from him until there's half the office between us.

"That's quite the view you have there. It's a good reminder of who you should be with." He tells me, amusement thick in his tone.

I shake my head at him. "I beg to differ. Now, unfortunately, I'm not available for lunch today or any day for that matter. You should go."

I cross my arms over my chest and glare harder but he just nods and moves to drop into a visitor chair.

"Alright, let's talk here then."

The urge to screech in frustration barrels through me but instead I tamp it down and move back behind my desk, using it like a shield and settle slowly into my chair.

"I told Jude and I'll tell you the same, and please, share it with the other two if they have plans to ambush me. There…is…nothing…to…talk…about! We had a brief fling years ago in college that went bad. End of story. I don't know why all of a sudden you've all decided to try and rope me back in but it's not going to happen. So you all need to move the fuck on!"

My temper spikes at the end causing me to curse and I hate that I'm starting to lose the control I work so hard at keeping. Tate leans over and rests his hard, muscle-roped arms on my desk and hits me with an intense stare.

"Not all of a sudden, Savy. It never went away. We fucked up that night, a hundred percent, but we knew it almost as soon as it happened. We chased after you but missed you by minutes when you got on that plane. There was nothing we could do right then. We had the playoffs and then nationals back to back. All of us texted you, called you, left messages trying to explain."

I shake my head and scoff, turning my face away so I don't have to look at him.

"Not all of you," falls from my lips unwittingly and I bite down hard on my tongue until I taste blood. Tate sighs and leans back into the chair.

"That's on him to fix. But you can't blame the rest of us for his mistakes. Savy, we thought you'd come back when school started again. We thought we had time to fix it, to show you how much we wanted you and how sorry we were for that moment of doubt that ruined everything. But you didn't come back and then the draft happened and Jude and I were sent to opposite sides of the country."

He pushes a hand through his hair, his brows crashing together over hazel eyes swimming with regret.

"Do you know when I stepped onto that field for the first time as a professional football player I always thought it would be the best day of my life? I stood there, hearing the crowd cheering my name and I scanned as many faces as I could but it wasn't the best day…because you weren't there. The one person who I knew would be proud of me. It should have been the best day of my life but it wasn't because you weren't there, I was all alone." He tells me in a soft tone and I flinch back as memories take over.

I scrunch down further in my seat and tug the baseball cap lower until it bumps into my oversized sunglasses as the team takes the field. When they announce Tate's name and he turns to look at the crowd chanting his name, my heart forgets briefly of the pain he caused me as it swells with how proud I am of him. It was the same last week when I went to Jude's first game. These careless boys hurt me so badly but I had to come. I knew they wouldn't have family in the stands to support them on such a momentous moment and even though they will never know I was here, I couldn't stand the thought of them starting their careers with no one who loves them present.

Tate's wide grin starts dimming as he keeps looking through the crowd until his lips are in a flat line and then he lifts a hand in a brief wave and runs to join his team. I curse his shitty parents for not being here and causing Tate's joy to dim. I sit back and watch the rest of the game wondering how long it will be before I can finally let these men go and move on.

I focus back onto him, roll my lips in and bite down on them and then slide my eyes away to keep from telling him that I was there, that he wasn't alone, now that I know it was me he was looking for and not his parents.

"Baby, look at me."

As much as I don't want to, my eyes go back to him like magnets.

"I'll be the first to admit that I fucked up with you over and over again but I'm not that guy anymore. All of us were just a bunch of dumb twenty-year-olds with our heads stuck up our asses. We've all grown up since then. Please, give us…me…another chance to prove that."

I stare hard into his eyes as emotions crash over me but the main one is pain. I can't do this. I won't let him or Jude or any of them back in. It's been proven again and again that anyone I love leaves me. I will never let that happen again so I take a fortifying breath and push to my feet.

"I'm sorry, Tate, I have no more chances to give. I have a meeting so you need to go."

He stands but doesn't move for a few moments just stares at me and then nods. "I understand I used up all my chances with you but please, Savy, don't shut out Jude. He…needs you. He never stopped believing in you and loving you."

With another nod, Tate walks out of my office and closes the door behind him softly.

I crash back into my chair, wrap my arms around my stomach and just try to hold back the pain that seeing them and hearing their words has reignited.

"Miss Sevan? You have a meeting with Mr. Hanson in five minutes."

Mandy's voice comes through my intercom to remind me that I have responsibilities here so I suck the pain back in and bury it deep. I push to my feet, close my eyes for a moment and let my mask settle into place then grab the stack of folders and head to Mark's office. I catch the flash of annoyance that crosses his expression before his charming smile erases it.

"Savanna, I hope you had a good weekend. The picture I saw of you at Stella's opening was a surprise. I didn't know you had started seeing someone."

I send him a tight smile, shake my head and brush it off.

"I'm not. You know how the press can spin things. Listen, we need to talk about these deals you've been making." I lift the stack of folders and sink into a chair across from him. "We talked about this and agreed that we wouldn't go in this direction. Mark, I don't understand why you would sign them anyway. None of these deals forward the Sevan Corporation in the direction we want to go. If anything, it sets us back."

He leans back in his chair and steeples his hands with a soft smile. "Princess, you've come a long way in the last four years but you're still so young. The men I made those deals with have a long history with Sevan. There are expectations that need to be met. This is how business works. A favor for a favor. You'll learn that in time."

My fingers tighten on the stack of folders at the condescension in his tone.

"This is nothing but greed! These deals do nothing but circle the wealth around to the same old families who don't need more. The exact purpose of the Sevan Corporation we've been working to change. I'm sorry but I can't sign off on these."

A hard look comes into his eyes before he looks away. "I understand your frustration but as I said, this is how business is done. We give to them and they give back. That's how we keep the coffers filled so the money can trickle down to those who need it. If you don't sign off on the promises I made, it will put many of our programs in jeopardy. Savanna, you have to trust me to know what's best for the Sevan Corporation."

I try not to growl in frustration and take a deep breath. "I do trust you, Mark, but I disagree with this completely. Our coffers, as you put it, are more than filled. They are overflowing. There are other, cleaner avenues for us to explore. I'm not going to sign off on deals that make already obscenely wealthy men even richer as those in need get a 'trickle' of what they need. When I fired the board and made you CEO, we had a plan to change all that. So why the backpedaling now?"

Mark pushes to his feet, forcing me to look up at him and it gives me a sour taste in the back of my mouth so I push to mine. I can see by his expression he's not going to concede so I extend an olive branch to my father's best friend and the only family

I have left. I hold out the files to him until he takes them.

"If you're set on this course, you need to show me why. 'That's how business is done' isn't good enough. Put together a report detailing how this benefits the Sevan Corporation other than just adding more zeros to our bank balance and what the ramifications would be if these deals are canceled. I won't sign off otherwise."

His brows crash together and he barks, "I've been running this Corporation for a long time!"

I snap right back. "And I OWN it!"

I suck in a breath and run a hand down my ponytail to try to calm myself. I'm not being fair to him. Having the guys ambush me has set me on edge and I'm taking it out on Mark. I send him a softer smile and try again.

"I'm sorry for that, Mark. I truly am trying to understand why we would make these deals. I'm just asking for you to walk me through it so we can get on the same page. Will you please help me?"

All the anger fades from his face as he sets the folders on his desk with a nod. "Of course, princess. I'm sorry as well. I'll have a report for you in the next few weeks and we'll go over it line by line until you're satisfied."

We share strained smiles but when I leave his office, that smile drops away completely and is replaced by a frown.

TATE

I punch the code into the gate as my breathing starts to slow from the six-mile run I just finished. I walk up the long driveway to the house we all went in on when we relocated here a month ago. I scan the mansion as it comes into view and huff a laugh at how different it is from the last house we all shared. It's around eleven thousand square feet different and a hell of a lot more zeros on the price tag. I thought being all together again, we would slide right back into the family unit we used to be but it's not the same. Something is missing that makes me feel like we're all holding our breath and I know without a doubt what's missing is Savy. It's not going to feel like a real home until she's in it.

We need her to come back to us and smooth all the jagged edges that have developed between us all. Ash and Jude still aren't back to what they used to have and Beck, well Beck needs her forgiveness more than all of us to move on. With or without her.

I find Jude in the massive chef's kitchen throwing together a stir-fry, bobbing along to a Lizzo song and it brings me to a stop in the doorway with a grin forming. It's the first time I've seen the old playful Jude that he used to be since she left us. When Savy didn't come back, it was like she stole all the crazy fun Jude had in him. He got real dark for a while there until a year ago when his focus became more determined than ever to get her back.

"Do my hair toss, check my…"

He screeches as he pretends to whip long hair over his shoulder and comes to a stop when he sees me watching.

"Hey T, didn't see you this morning. Whatcha up to?"

I move to the sub-zero fridge and snag a water bottle, crack it, and down half before answering him.

"I went into the city. Went to see her."

The spatula in his hand freezes for a moment before giving the stir-fry one more toss and then shutting off the heat and turning to me with cautious eyes.

"How did it go? How was she?"

I cap the water bottle and run the coolness of it over the back of my neck.

"She's…harder…than she used to be. Physically, it's like all the softness she used to have was burned away but it just makes her even more beautiful. Honestly, she looked tired."

"Hmm, if she's not sleeping that means something's weighing on her. Or someone is."

I nod. "Yeah, she shut me down pretty quick. Told me she doesn't have any more chances to give. Also told me to tell the others not to bother ambushing her because she's not interested."

Jude leans against the counter and rubs at his mouth but when he looks back up at me, he has a smirk on his face.

"Too bad baby doll's not running this show anymore. She can say she's not interested as much as she wants to but she's lying. Savy's over us as much as we're over her."

I push back my sweaty hair as doubts fill me. "I don't know, man. She was pretty clear this morning."

He barks a laugh, turns, and dumps his lunch on a plate. "You want to know what I'm sure of?" I cock a brow so he tells me. "Orange and blue. Yesterday morning, when I jumped her fence, she wasn't wearing black. She was wearing my old blue Cannon's t-shirt and your orange Hennessy Academy hoodie. Nah, if our girl was over us, she wouldn't be sleeping in our clothes. We ain't letting up T. This was just the opening shot."

The thought of Savy wearing my hoodie after all this time has a warm glow filling my chest so I square my shoulders with a nod.

"Alright, we ramp it up then." I look around the room and ask, "Where's Ash and Beck?"

"Ash started that exchange thing with the ortho department at the hospital today. He'll be working out of there for the next week. Beck went to the zoo."

I swipe a piece of broccoli from his plate with a quick dodge. "I'm gonna hit the shower. Let's make a plan on what's next when the others get back later."

Jude waves his fork at me in agreement in between shoveling forkfuls of stir-fry into his mouth.

When I step under the heat of the water and tip my head back and let myself get lost in the fantasy of what life will look like when my baby girl is finally back in my arms.

SAVY

I stand at the back door with an angry scowl. Mo is vibrating at my feet to be let out and I'm considering trading him in for a vicious dog breed that would rip apart the intruder waiting for me in my backyard. This is the third morning in a row that Jude's been out there waiting on me and I'm starting to lose my mind a little bit. The first two days, I just let Mo out and slammed the door behind him and then hid in an upstairs room that faced the rear to watch him throw a ball for Mo for an hour before he finally gave up and hopped back over the wall and left. I've googled companies that will install spikes or glass shards on top of the wall but so far haven't been able to bring myself to make a call to have it done.

I chew on my thumbnail for a few moments as I stare out at Jude and the 'I dare you' look on his face as he stares back but when Mo whines and shuffles letting me know he has to go out soon or make a mess on my floor, I cave with a growl. I throw the door open and stomp out. Mo makes a dash for the closest bit of lawn and Jude beams at me.

"Good morning, baby doll. Back to black?"

I ignore his greeting and his comment on the black silk pajamas I've forced myself to start wearing instead of his shirt and launch right into my rant.

"Enough! Stop coming here, Jude! I don't want you and if you force my hand, I'll increase security to keep you out."

He tilts his head and lifts the take-out cup he brought toward me.

"Haven't had your coffee yet, huh?"

I stomp my foot and let out a small screech. "What the fuck do you want from me?"

He pushes to his feet, the grin fading to an intense look.

"Every…fucking…thing. I want everything from you, doll, and I'm not giving up until you give it to me."

I scoff and toss my hair back, annoyed that I didn't put it up before coming downstairs again this morning.

"I already gave you that and you and the others shit all over it! Fuck you, Jude. I have nothing to give to you or anyone!" I yell at him.

He strides toward me like a hunter stalking his prey and a shiver races up my back as my breathing picks up.

He gets right up into my face and grinds out, "Bull…shit. Bullshit, Savy. You didn't give me everything. You gave me a fucking peek over the wall you hide behind. A small glimpse of who you really are and it made me fall head over heels in love with you." He thrusts a finger at the back garden wall. "That's just the first one I had to scale to get to you. I know the real one is the one you've wrapped around yourself and it's going to be a lot harder to scale but, doll, it could take ten fucking years and I'd still keep climbing to get to that glimpse I saw back then."

I suck in a tortured breath and his eyes drop to my mouth before he yanks me against his chest and slams his lips against mine. Four and a half years of pent-up emotion, pain, and desire flood out as our tongues clash and battle. My fingers are clawed into his shirt and his are digging into my back and hip hard enough to leave bruises and it still doesn't feel like enough. He growls and nips at my bottom lip as I moan and pull at his shirt but then Mo's big head butts into us, making me stagger to the side. He drops a slobbered cover ball at Jude's feet and hits him with those big brown pleading eyes.

I take two steps back and drag my hands through my long hair as my brain clears from the Jude bomb that just hit me. He reaches down to pick up the ball and throws it to the other end of the yard and then curses when he looks back at me.

"No, don't, baby. Stay with me."

But I'm already shaking my head and closing myself off. "You need to go. There's nothing I can give you, Jude. Four years, ten years, it wouldn't matter. There's nothing to give, nothing to see. I don't want you."

Mo comes back and drops the ball so he throws it again. "That kiss didn't feel like nothing to me, doll."

I roll my eyes at him. "It's just physical, nothing more."

He steps right back up to me and tilts my chin up.

"I'll fucking take it, then."

"I…what?"

He chuckles darkly. "We both felt that. The need coursing through our bodies? That's a forest without rain for four long years just waiting for a spark to ignite it. You want to keep your wall up? Keep your heart from me? Fine, I'll accept that for now but I fucking told you, doll. This body right here, it's mine. I also told you I'm not going anywhere so you'll give it to me. You'll let me do all the wicked, filthy things I've dreamed about doing to it for the last four years because, baby, you need it just as bad as I do."

I press my thighs together as my core clenches hard in agreement. I try to keep my eyes hard and full of denial but a slow smile crosses his face as his hand comes up and his knuckles drag over one of my peaked nipples that is pressing hard against the silk of my shirt, showing just how bad I do.

"And I'm going to give it to you."

He stoops down lightning fast to scoop up the ball and throw it again, sends me a wink, and then he's up and over the garden wall. I turn and walk back to the house trying hard to ignore the soaked silk between my legs.

An hour later Patrick sees me to the door of my office building. My head is still so filled with Jude that I walk straight into a hard body but before I can bounce off strong hands grip my elbows and steady me in my heels. A small chuckle has my head snapping up.

"Morning, baby girl. I'd tell you to watch where you're going but I like the results when you don't."

"For the love of…What do you want, Tate?"

I grind out and push myself away from him. He smiles with soft eyes, shakes his head, and steps back.

"I'm good now, baby girl. Just wanted to start my day by seeing your beautiful face. Enjoy your day."

I stand in the middle of the busy lobby as people go past and around me and watch him slide through the crowd and out the revolving doors without looking back. I'm at a complete loss for what to do next. Fuck.

I'm next to useless for the rest of the day. Every time I try to focus on work, my mind circles back to Tate and Jude. The things they said ricochet around my head like marbles in a pinball machine. My body is wound tight with the feelings of wanting another's touch that I've long since buried. No one has touched me but myself that way since I walked away from them and my libido is thrashing in backlash. I shove away from my desk as the walls start to feel like they're closing in on me and fly out of my office to haunt the halls. Mandy sends me a curious look but I ignore her and keep going, looking to burn off some of this frustration. I stop in at a few departments to touch base but never settle anywhere for long and finally decide to hit the executive staff room for a drink and a snack to try and settle the angst in my stomach.

I turn down the corridor toward the staff room but just as I go past the supply closet the door opens and a hand bites into my arm to jerk me into the darkness of it. Another hand is pressed over my mouth as I try to scream and then the door clicks closed, putting me in complete darkness. I start to thrash but a low chuckle has me freezing in place. The strong hands spin me around and my chest is pressed against the shelves as his chest presses against my back.

His mouth skims down my neck with a hot breath making my whole body shake.

"Every goddamn night since you left, I fisted my aching cock and stroked it to the memories of this curvy, hot body, doll. The things I did to you in my head to punish you for leaving me? There was no way I was going another fucking day without having the taste of you on my tongue."

His hand slides off my mouth down to wrap around my throat. I want to yell, cry out, demand to know how he made it up to my floor past security but his other hand wraps around one of my thighs and starts to slide up stealing any words I could say.

"Put your hands on the shelves, baby, and hold fucking tight."

My hands snap up to grip the metal even as my mind screams at what a weak, pathetic woman I am but my body's overruling all thought now as those hard, rough fingers slide under my skirt. He groans into my neck as they brush over the lace band of my stocking and hit bare skin. My teeth bite down into my bottom lip to stop the whine of need escaping but my ass pushes back against the hardness pressing against me. He pushes the scrap of silk coving my mound to the side and brushes lightly against my slit. A choked groan heats the skin of my neck at what he finds.

"Fucking soaked, baby. Still so fucking responsive to touch. I'm going to make this pussy weep so bad it'll forget any other man's touch but mine." He drags his teeth up my neck to bite my earlobe. "No other man gets to touch this now, doll. This pussy is mine, mine and my brothers', and no one else. Say it!" He growls against my ear.

I know what he really wants. He wants me to tell him that there never has been anyone else. Well, fuck him. He wants to play? I can fucking play right back.

I shrug against him causing his fingers to slip into my folds exactly where I want them. He punishes me for not saying what he wants in the best fucking way when two of those fingers thrust deep inside my throbbing channel. I clamp down on them trying to suck them even deeper and he spits out a strangled, "Fu-ck!"

He uses those fingers inside me to drag me back harder against his cock, grinding hard against my ass and I laugh. I laugh because he thinks he's in control of my body but the truth is, I've got a collar and leash on his just as bad. The laugh turns into a moan as he slams those curled fingers into me again and again while grinding the heel of his palm against my clit. The wave he built starts to spike and my pussy starts to pulse, so fucking close to the peak and then he pulls out and steps back from me causing a gasp of denial to gush from between my panting lips.

"See you real soon, baby doll." He growls out and then a wash of light hits me before the door closes and I'm back in the dark again.

My clit throbs and my fingers curl against the metal shelves but a wide grin spreads across my face. He has no fucking clue that I'm not the same little innocent I was when he first put his hands on me. I might have locked my heart away for good but a girl has needs and after years of experimenting with toys I know exactly how I like it so I finish myself off quickly without his help. I straighten up, smooth my skirt back down after arranging my underwear back into place and lift my chin. My mind is no longer clouded and confused. I will never let him or the others cause me more emotional damage but sex? If Jude thinks he can control me, manipulate me - by heating me up and leaving me wanting? He has no idea how hot I can make things for him too. The question is if he'll survive my burn.

JUDE

Fuck, baby doll grew some teeth. My sweet little girl isn't the same as she used to be. I slam my fist into the punching bag over and over again but it does nothing to distract me from the ache in my cock and my heart. I told her I'd take the physical when she denied me anything more hoping it would be a pathway to cracking that fucking wall she hides behind but instead, she filled a moat around it with napalm.

She fucking laughed! It was like she knew exactly what I wanted to hear from her and that little shrug instead of an answer had me being rougher with her than I should have been. But my doll just got even hotter and wetter because of it. My girl likes it rough and it makes me wonder who the fuck taught her that. Savy was so fucking ripe for the picking back then. Every damn thing I did to her, taught her, she took to like an angel. I had barely scratched the surface with her when shit went bad. Four fucking years is a long time for a girl that responsive to touch to go without it. I'd be a fool to think she hasn't had any experiences along the way. Just because I never allowed another woman to touch me doesn't mean she never allowed another man to touch her. It makes me want to paint a knife red from any fucker that laid his hands on what's mine.

"FUCK!"

I punch the bag one more time with all the pent-up anger and frustration inside of me then hit the showers to sake the other frustration I can't shake since leaving her in that room on the edge. I picture those pink fucking lips of hers wrapped around my cock while she looks up at me with tear-filled blue eyes and paint the tiles with my release. I step under the hot spray and tip my head back as a grin takes over my face.

Alright, alright, alright. I'll just have to turn the heat up a bit more. I'll destroy the foundation of her fucking wall brick by brick until the whole thing comes crashing down. She loved me once, I know she did. I can make her fall again.

SAVY

I don't know if it's relief or not when I peek out my back window Friday morning and don't see Jude in his now regular spot at my patio table. I blow out a breath and call Mo to follow me downstairs to be let out. His big feet thump to the floor when he scrambles off the bed and then gallops past me down the stairs like a small pony. I crack the back door to let him out and smile as he barrels through with a deep warning bark to any birds that might have dared enter his kingdom. I go to pull the door closed but the knob is ripped from my hand as Jude steps around it. He steps through, crowding me back, and shuts it behind him. His golden eyes are fierce with need as I step back away from him but he snags the silk of my sleep shirt and drags me back.

"Never got that taste I wanted, doll. Here to rectify that," he says gruffly and then his knees hit the floor in front of me and my loose pajama pants are whipped down. He lifts one of my legs and then the other and tosses them aside leaving me with just a pair of black cheeky panties peaking out from under my shirt. Panties that are already getting damp. He looks up at me with an expression daring me to tell him to stop so I just arch a brow with my own 'get on with it look'.

Amusement lights his eyes as he accepts the challenge and then his rough hands are sliding up my thighs, fingers spread so his thumbs brush over my center.

I tug my shirt tight against my stomach so I can watch what he's going to do to me, earning a humming laugh from him. He moves in closer and then his tongue sweeps out to tease my panty line. My clit starts to throb in anticipation but he keeps licking me through my panties, never finding the spot I need most. That's when I realize he's here to punish, tease, wind me up again and leave me desperate for more of him and I'm not having it. It's my fucking turn to play.

I slide my fingers up past his fade into the longer white-blond hair on top and yank trying to angle him where I want him but he holds firm against me making me bite back a laugh. So instead, I lift one leg like I'm going to put it over his shoulder but jam my knee against it instead and shove hard putting him on his ass at my feet. I follow him down and pin his shoulders with both my knees and smirk right fucking back at him. My drenched underwear is inches from his face in this position but not close enough for him to lift his head to get his mouth on me. I keep the pressure on his shoulders to keep him in place and drag a hand back over his t-shirt-covered abs until I can slide right under the waistband of his joggers and boxers and then I wrap my fingers around his hot, throbbing cock. Jude freezes under me as his mouth falls open and his eyes squeeze closed, a harsh, "Baby?" slipping out.

I let my fingers trace over each one of the barbells pierced through his hard shaft and then squeeze again. I take my free hand and drag it down between my breasts pushing my shirt tails aside and then slip them under my panties and into the wet heat between my legs. Jude's head comes up and his eyes zero in on the movement hidden behind the cotton. He groans a desperate sound so I start stroking his cock into a steady rhythm that matches what I'm doing to my pussy.

"Fuck, doll. Let me do…let me fucking see it at least?"

I tip my head back, moaning as I hit the perfect spot. After four years I know exactly how to make my body sing, fast or drawn out real slow. Judging by the warm precum slicking my fingers around him, this needs to be fast.

"Shut up, working here," I tell him.

A choked laugh comes from him as his fingertips brush against the outside of my thighs, the only place he can reach with him pinned down. He hisses in frustration and then starts bucking his hips up to fuck my hand so I squeeze the heavy weight of him tighter and thrust my fingers deeper into my pussy, biting back the cry as everything tightens right up and starts to pulse. It's exactly the right timing because Jude swells in my hand. Our cries mix as we both fall together. Him surging his hips higher and me grinding down on his chest to ride out the pleasure on my fingers. When my head finally falls forward and meets his eyes the awe and love in them have me jerking my hand from his pants. I bring it forward as I pull the other from my pussy and show him how wet it is, hovering my wet fingers close to his lips for a moment. But I snatch them away and slick them against his cum on my other hand and then flatten my tongue and swipe it up to lick off our combined tastes. His head bounces back against the hardwood floor with a groan.

"Fucking Christ, baby."

I shake my head at him. "No. That wasn't Christ and it wasn't you. That was all fucking me…baby."

I turn my feet under me and push up to rise off of him and step away but he wraps a loose hand around my ankle stopping me so I look down at him with a blank expression, mask firmly in place.

"Doll…Savy, I love you so fucking much."

The power of it in his eyes tells me it's true but that's not happening so I arch a brow.

"You should be careful with that. There's a big difference between burning and getting burnt, Jude. You can let yourself out. I have to get to work."

I hear his head bang on the floor again but I don't look back as I climb the stairs.

By the time I come down, showered and dressed for work, Jude's gone and Mo's shoveling back his breakfast like it'll be his last meal. Once he's done, I give him scratches and squeezes of love, roll the lint roller over my dress and suit jacket and promise him a cuddle-fest when I get home tonight.

I stride into the building with my chin up and Jude Dixon firmly tucked away at the back of my mind only to stumble to a stop when Tate steps in front of me for the second morning in a row. I don't bother speaking this time, I just wait him out and get a flash of dimples when he grins and ducks his head. He holds out a small box for me and without thinking, my hand comes up to take it.

"What is this?' I snap.

His hand comes up and smooths down my ponytail hanging over my shoulder.

"Just something sweet for my sweetheart. You look beautiful today. I hope you have a great day."

And then he steps around me and walks on by. I try to stop myself but my heels turn as I track him through the lobby and out the door but this time, he glances back just before he reaches it and sends me a wink. For the first time in years, I feel a hot blush start to slide up my neck into my cheeks. I whip around and storm to the elevator, all the confidence and swagger I felt when I stepped into the building a few minutes ago gone.

I can't stop glaring at the pink box in my hand as I ride up and I almost smash the thing with how tight I'm holding it. I finally flip the top of it open and glare at the perfectly frosted cupcake inside with a chocolate heart at the tip. When my feet carry me past Mandy's desk, her head pops up with a frown bringing me to a stop.

"What? What is it?"

She sends me a sympathetic look before telling me, "Um, the lawyers called. They need you at their office at two for a meeting."

My brows crash together in confusion. Our lawyers come to us. Why would they need me to go to their building?

"I'm very sorry, Miss Sevan. It's about your stepmother and sister."

Never has it been harder to keep my mask in place as my blood pressure skyrockets and nausea starts churning in my stomach. I give her a curt nod and move to step past but stop and extend my hand to her. She takes the pink box from me with a small curious smile.

"For your break. Enjoy, Mandy."

And then I quietly shut my office door behind me.

SAVY

I force all thoughts of Jude, Tate, and the upcoming meeting from my head to bury myself in work, downing three pain relievers to try and stop the headache that the buried stress causes. It flares back to life as I step out of the SUV in front of a skyscraper filled with floor after floor of law offices. My mind keeps going around and around on what these women could possibly want after I severed all ties to them four years ago. As I step into the elevator, I scoff. Whatever they want, it will have to do with money. That's all I ever was to them after my dad died. An ATM to use and an unwanted child to bully. I dig my nails into my palms while my head throbs, my stomach knots itself in anxiety, and memories of the last time I was across a boardroom table from them surge forward.

"I really don't understand why we needed to be here for this!"

Celeste whines as she and Vanessa take their seats across from the law team that's handled my father's affairs since his death. I stand next to the windows looking out with my arms crossed over my stomach trying to contain the ache inside. I can't bear to even look at Vanessa without remembering that night a week ago when she destroyed any chance I had for happiness.

"This is ridiculous! Vanessa and I were supposed to be on the jet right now on the way to the Maldives for the holidays. There's absolutely no reason we have to be here for Savanna to sign this paperwork."

One of the lawyers clears his throat. "Yes, well, this is more than just Miss Sevan taking ownership of her inheritance. There are matters to go over with both of you as well. Miss Sevan? If you could join us, we'll begin."

I drag in a deep breath, straighten my shoulders and move to a chair across from Celeste but keep my eyes down.

"As you know, Miss Sevan has turned twenty-one and now controls the entirety of the Sevan holdings. At the time of her father's death, you and your daughter had not been listed in his will. You assumed guardianship of his minor daughter with the agreement that all your expenses would be covered for the duration. That has now come to an end with Miss Sevan coming into the full inheritance."

Celeste sucks in a sharp breath and I can see her lean forward in her seat from the corner of my eye.

"Wait one minute! What do you mean that's come to an end? As in, our expenses will no longer be covered? Don't be absurd!"

The lawyer continues like she didn't just interrupt him. "It was stipulated that you would receive a bulk payment for what was agreed upon in your pre-nuptial contract. However, after an audit was performed on your expenses since taking guardianship of Miss Sevan, it was determined that your personal expenses more than doubled that amount."

Celeste begins to jerk her hands and sputter. "Those expenses were to ensure Savanna continued the life she was accustomed to!"

Once again, the lawyer cuts her off. "The detailed audit showed that the money was not spent on Miss Sevan. All her clothing, food, and necessities were covered by the household budget already in place. No, the money you spent went exclusively to your and your daughter's travel, clothing, art purchases, and other extravagances. The auditors were unable to find any expenses that directly pertained to Miss Sevan. In short, you have defrauded the estate."

"Savanna! How can you let them say such things?" She asks me shrilly. "After everything I did for you? I could have left you all alone but instead I took you in as my own daughter!"

My head finally comes up at that with a deep frown. "You took me in? The minute they released me from the hospital you and Vanessa took the jet to the Bahamas. You left a broken, traumatized, grieving child all alone with no one but the staff to care for." I shake my head. "You didn't take me in. You just took. You've never done anything for me but make me feel like a burden… like I was never good enough for you or anyone to love."

Celeste shoves to her feet. "How can you say that? We're your family!"

My eyes slide toward Vanessa, who's glaring at me. "No, you aren't, you never were and your daughter took any chance I had at having one."

Vanessa barks out a bitter laugh with a toss of her blond hair. "You should be thanking me! That guy is a psychopath," she spits out. "He held a knife to my throat and threatened to kill me!"

My brows furrow hearing that. If that actually happened, it would have been Jude who did it for some reason. It doesn't matter now anyway so my gaze slides down to her perfectly unmarred skin and I shrug.

"But did you die?"

Her face turns a deep red. "You fucking cunt! I'll…"

"What did you do?" Celeste screams at her.

"I will have security remove you!" Yells one of my lawyers.

And I just rub between my eyes and snap, "Give her the check and let this be over."

Vanessa and Celeste cut off mid-rant and their eyes snapped back to the lawyer.

"Miss Sevan, against counsel's advice, has generously decided to pay you the sum of the original prenup amount and not pursue fraud charges against you as is her right. However, there are conditions. You must hand over all banking and credit cards. You will vacate her properties and sign nondisclosure agreements. You will never speak publicly about Miss Sevan to anyone or we will revisit the fraud charges and sue you both for every penny spent. Neither one of you are to contact Miss Sevan again in any way and should you meet at a public event, you are to keep your distance."

Both Vanessa and Celeste glare at me but I hold their gaze with a blank expression until Celeste snaps.

"Fine! Once again, you are a complete disappointment to me, Savanna. Your father would be ashamed of you to know how you've treated us."

I can't help but roll my eyes at that as I wave them out of the room. I have to believe that my dad would have seen through this viper and divorced her before they made it to their third wedding anniversary. Half the team herds the women from the room but the man next to me places a hand on my arm when I begin to rise.

"Miss Sevan, there's one more thing. Now that all the paperwork has been signed, I was instructed to give you this."

He slides an envelope across to me. I recognize my dad's loopy handwriting of my name on the front and suck in a breath.

"What…what is it?" I ask as I trace my fingers over my name.

"I believe it is a letter from your father. He gave it to us shortly after he married your stepmother with instructions to give it to you on your twenty-first birthday should he pass away before you reached it."

I pick it up and press it against my chest but I know that just like the messages I can't read from the men I thought might love me, I won't be able to read this one either.

I step from the elevators with my mask firmly in place, hiding all the turmoil inside of me and follow a secretary deeper into the floor to thankfully, a different meeting room than the last one I was in.

Celeste is sitting alone on one side of the large table with four lawyers across from her and a small amount of tension bleeds away knowing I won't have to see Vanessa too. I'd like to say she has no power over me but even after all this time, the pain from the damage she did that night still haunts me. I take a seat and lift a brow at Celeste.

"We had an agreement that there would be no contact. What could possibly make you risk the repercussions of breaking that, Celeste?"

I watch her swallow hard and dart glances at the lawyers before her eyes come back to rest on me again.

"It might be best if we had this conversation in private, Savanna."

"No. Say what you have to say." I tell her in a flat tone.

She twists her fingers and gives me a jerking nod. "First, I…I've had time to think about how I…we…treated you over the years and I felt the need to apologize to you. When your father died, I was so very upset that I…"

I cut her off with a sharp slap against the table. She doesn't get to make excuses for what she did to me as a child or all the years after.

"If this is why you interrupted my day then this meeting is over."

I start to rise from my chair but she throws up a hand to stop me. The apologetic expression is melting away as her lips purse like she just sucked on a lemon.

"Wait! Fine, cards on the table, then. There are things you don't know about that would affect your future. Things that would shock you to know and would change the course of how you go forward."

I narrow my eyes at her. "And? These things, you'll tell me?"

I spot the caginess slide into her eyes and huff out a bitter laugh. "For a price, right? You'll tell me for another payout."

I shake my head and move to stand, done with this blatant money grab but she jumps to her feet with her hands held out in a plea.

"Wait! Savanna, please. I really do have important information you'll want to know. It's just…I've taken a few missteps…financially. Your sis…Vanessa hasn't made things easy. Please, if you could just…"

"No. Not one more dime. I don't believe for a second you have anything to tell me that's not lies. You don't care about me, you never have. So, no. There will be no more money, now or ever."

Frustration has her mouth pinching closed but when I move to leave again, she yelps out, "Mark! It's about Mark."

I narrow my eyes at her and start shaking my head. There's nothing she could tell me about Mark that I don't already know. It was the lawyers in this very room that advised me to run a deep background on him before I made him the CEO after firing the board. I know about the women he sees. I know about the men's club he likes to frequent and the occasional trips to Vegas. None of that is out of line for a single man his age and it's not any of my business. There's nothing she could tell me about Mark worth a payout. It's just one more way she's trying to hurt me so I look down at the lead lawyer and nod.

"Have security escort her out if she refuses to leave. If she tries to contact you again, proceed with the fraud case you built."

I don't bother looking at Celeste again as I stride for the door but it's impossible to miss hearing her parting shot.

"You're going to regret this, Savanna!"

SAVY

I stand waiting for the elevator on shaky legs. As hard as I try to put all the years with Celeste and Vanessa behind me, I can't help but probe at those memories like a wound that never quite heals. Every time they left me alone for holidays, every harsh word, every way they made me feel worthless rears its ugly head. I just wanted a family, someone to love me. What's wrong with me that no one ever stays, I ask myself as I step into the elevator, lost in pitiful thoughts.

Emotions I shouldn't be feeling are way too close to the surface and I know it's because of Jude and Tate and the way they've been messing with my head. It was one thing to ignore the text messages, the letters sent that are stacked up in a drawer unopened and all the small gifts and flowers sent over the years but seeing them face to face, being forced to hear their words and now Jude's hands on my body has me completely off kilter. I stare straight ahead as the doors close and try hard not to cry for all the things I can't have. I closed my heart to the idea of a family, of love when…

I jerk my arm away when something warm and soft grabs my hand. My eyes practically bug out of my head when I look down and see a small boy that can't be much older than three or four years old. I give myself whiplash spinning my head around searching the elevator for a mom or dad that I must have missed in my oblivion and come up empty. I press my hand against my forehead checking to see if I'm in a fevered delirium because what the hell is a tiny human doing alone in an elevator in a building full of lawyers?

A tug on my skirt has me shaking off my astonishment and crouching down to get on this adorable little man's level. He has soft brown curls, pretty light blue eyes framed by dark lashes, and chubby pink cheeks that I want to smother with kisses.

"Hi there, sweet boy. Where's your mama?"

All I get back from him is a small smile. He must be in the building with his family for something and got away from them. His mother must be frantic with worry.

"Okay, don't worry, sweetheart, I'll take you down to security and have you back in your mommy's arms in no time." I brush back some of his curls with a soft smile and ask, “Can you tell me your name? My name is Savy.”

His beautiful eyes light up and then he’s lifting his little arms in the universal little kid way of asking to be picked up. I hesitate briefly. This isn’t my child to be picking up but I know if he was mine and he was lost and alone I would be happy to have a kind stranger take care of him until he was returned to me. I lift him carefully like he’s made of glass and almost swoon when the little charmer tucks his face into my neck and melts against me in that trusting boneless way only tiny kids do.

The elevator stops at different floors as people get on and off on its way down but I’m completely lost to the silky softness of his hair against my cheek and the sweet smell of it. He smells like grass and sunshine with a hint of baby shampoo. My heart aches painfully holding someone else’s child and wishing desperately that he was mine. To have a child of my own, to love and be loved so completely back has my eyes crashing closed as I rest my head gently on what I’ll never have in sorrow.

The elevator bounces slightly to a stop on the ground floor and I stay put, dragging out the dream of this for a few seconds more, letting the other passengers get off first. I place a barely there kiss on his soft curls, open my eyes and move to step out only to come to a quick stop at the man holding the doors open with a frantic look on his face. I stare back at Beckett Hart in bewilderment for a few beats until the tiny boy in my arms straightens up with a huge grin and speaks for the first time.

"Daddy! ***Sa***-vy!"

He pats my cheek with his warm little hand and leans away from me with his arms out to Beckett. I didn't know it was possible for a heart to break a second time. The little lost angel is Beckett's son. Beck has a son and that means…

"Savy? Fuck, I can explain…"

It takes everything I have but I cut him off, trying to keep my voice as steady as possible as a trapped sob pulses painfully in my chest but it still comes out broken in pieces anyway.

"I…I found…him. He's, he's okay. Your wife must be terrified right now but he's okay."

I try to slide past him but he shifts to block me.

"No, Savy, it's not…"

I can't, I can't! I'm going to crack and I can't do that here with so many people to see it.

I shake my head quickly and whisper, "He's so, so beautiful, Beck. I…I'm happy for y-you."

And then I push past him and almost run across the lobby to get out, to get away as another piece of me dies.

BECKETT

"Hey, man! Can we get on or is this your personal elevator?"

The words jar me from the daze of what just happened and I quickly step aside with Tanner in my arms so the people waiting can get on the elevator. My heart is racing still from the panic of losing sight of my son and the terror of not knowing where he was. My arms tighten around the little escape artist as I blow out a nerve-filled breath. All it took was a split second. I turned back to answer a question from my lawyer and he was gone. I spotted the elevator doors closing and his cheeky grin through the gap a second too late to stop it from happening.

I press my lips against his hair and walk us over to where his nanny waits with the stroller. Jesus, I think that might have taken a decade off my life. He was only gone for the time it took for the elevator to reach the lobby and thank fuck the one I jumped in beat it down or this could have gone a very different way. I left the nanny, Paula, down here in the lobby for our last mediation appointment wanting to keep the final details of the arrangement private but I should have just had her come up and wait in the law firm's lobby instead. This is just one more way that I'm screwing up as a father and I sink onto the bench beside Paula with shaky legs as the adrenalin bleeds off.

"Savy, Daddy! Savy!"

Tanner yells in his high-pitched voice and I want to cry right here and now but I can't do that in front of my son so instead I paste on a smile and nod.

"Yeah, you found her, buddy. Listen, you can't run off like that, Tan! That scared Daddy a lot. You could have been lost. Something terrible could have happened to you."

He nods with a grin. "Yes! Savy!"

I sigh and let Paula get him into his stroller. My boy's been hearing Savy's name his whole life so it's not a surprise that he's excited to finally put a face to a name. What are the fucking odds that Savy would not only be in this building but find my son when he got himself lost? This was the complete opposite way that I wanted her to find out about him. Fuck! I scrub my hands over my face as I picture what I saw when those doors opened and everyone got off.

The last person I expected to see holding my son was Savy. Her eyes were closed as she rested her cheek against Tanner's head and the look of pure despondency on her face, like she truly believes she will never have her own child on top of the sheer relief at seeing my son safe, almost took my knees out. I never thought I would see her break again like she did that night four years ago. We're here to give her all the happiness and love she deserves and now I know I won't have any shot at making that happen. The look in her eyes when she said the word…wife? Fuck me.

I get Paula and Tanner down to the parking garage and strapped in and don't even curse at the wall-to-wall traffic as I listen to the wheels on the bus over and over again while Tanner sings his version of it with mismatched words. This wasn't supposed to go this way. I was supposed to have the chance to explain what happened, ask her for forgiveness, beg if I had to. I just needed one more day, today, to have the final paperwork signed off on by the courts and lawyers. I clench my fingers around the leather of the steering wheel as I remember the worst and best day of my life.

I hear the doorbell ring but ignore it knowing Ash is downstairs and will get it. I have an exam coming up and the contracts law portion of it is kicking my ass so I need all the study time I can get if I want to pass it.

"Beck! Get your ass down here on the double!"

Ash bellows up the stairs and there's something in his tone that has a shiver running down my back. I waste no time barreling out of my room down the stairs and find him and a woman I find vaguely familiar waiting for me in the living room. She's sitting on the edge of the couch with a mound of bags at her feet and one covered by a blanket. I scan her for a beat, trying to place where I know her from but it doesn't click until she leans over and her shirt gapes open showing me a large rose tattoo blooming out of her cleavage. Hazy, alcohol-soaked memories of a drunken night almost a year ago flit through my head and guilt crashes through me.

"Uh, hey. I, I'm sorry, I never got your name that night." I tell her with a grimace and wonder what the fuck she's doing here. She smirks and shrugs one shoulder.

"Yeah, not a lot of conversation happened that night. The only reason I even know yours is…" She tosses something at me and when I catch it see that it's my wallet that was stolen. I cock a what the fuck brow at her and she shrugs again with a small laugh.

"Right, sorry about that - but silver lining, at least I knew how to find you again."

I toss the wallet on the coffee table and cross my arms glaring at her. "And my phone? That went missing too."

She rolls her eyes at me and leans back on the couch. "Sold it for a few bucks. I'm sure a hotshot football player like you didn't have any hardship replacing it."

I shoot a look Ash's way and he returns a cringe-filled one so turn back to her. "Well, great. Thanks for returning the wallet but I have a feeling that's not why you're here, right?"

"Got it in one, big guy. Look, when I nail some guy at a party, it's always a game of Russian Roulette that I might come away with something undesirable. You know, like a case of gonorrhea or a black eye but I did not sign up for this shit. I gave it a month, you know, trying to do the right thing and all that bullshit but I'm done so it's all yours."

She pushes to her feet with a pissed-off look but I hold out my hand to stop her from walking out.

"Lady, I have no fucking clue what you're talking about. What's all mine?"

She purses her lips, scans me up and down, and then bends over and whips the blanket covering one of her bags off and everything inside my body goes still. I can't make sense of what I'm seeing here. There's the tiniest baby I've ever seen sleeping in a car seat at my feet and I can't force my mind to put the pieces together.

"Well, umm… good luck!"

She says with a laugh and starts walking around me. Thankfully Ash's head is still attached to his body because he grabs her and pushes her back onto the couch.

"Nice try, bitch. Sit your ass down and start talking. You're not going to drop a kid here and just walk away. Who says it's even his?"

She glares at Ash and then pulls a crumpled cigarette pack from her pocket and draws a bent one out and jams it between her lips.

"Fine. Mind if I smoke?"

Ash snags the smoke from her mouth and breaks it in two with a growl so she throws herself back against the couch cushions with a huff.

"Fuck you, man! Those are expensive. I don't got any money to buy more," she whines. "Fucking kid has eaten up all my damn cash. You need to take him

or he's going into the system. I got shit to do that doesn't include a kid hanging off my hip."

Ash drops a hand on my shoulder and squeezes but my eyes keep going back to the baby sleeping peacefully through his mother trying to give him away.

"How do we know the baby is his?"

She leans forward, looks at the baby, and then up at me and tosses her hands up. "Sure looks like him." She chuckles when Ash takes a hard step her way. "Easy there, tiger. I'm just kidding. The dates match up. You could say I had a dry spell for a few months and big boy here was the only guy I was with. Trust me, it's his kid. But if you don't want him, my next stop is the firehouse. They have that safe haven thing where you can drop off a kid no questions asked."

Ash throws a hand through his hair with a groan. "We're not trusting you with shit. We're going to need a birth certificate, a paternity test and…"

I block them out and crouch down to get a closer look at the child and see it's wearing a blue onesie thing with footballs on it. It's a boy. It's a boy and she says he's mine. My son, my family, mine. The baby's lips twitch into a smile in his sleep and two huge emotions war in my chest. Love surges with a fierce need to care for and protect him and grief throbs painfully on the other side knowing that I now will never get the woman I love back.

We finally clear downtown and get on the expressway toward home. With Tanner asleep in the back seat, I shut off the children's music and war with two more huge emotions once again. Relief that Tanner is finally all mine and heartache for hurting Savy and losing any chance I had to fix things. I don't know how I'm going to be able to stay with my brothers if they manage to convince Savy to give them another chance. Seeing her with them, being around her, and not being able to love her will slowly kill me.

The drive that should only have taken a half hour but ended up being three times that with traffic and construction finally comes to an end as I pull through our gates and up the drive. Jude bounds down the stairs with a fist full of balloons and a wide grin as he waits for me to open my door.

He loves Tanner just as much as I do and it's been a long, drawn-out battle to finally get Justine's money-grabbing hands off of him. Jude was the one who finally just threw out a number she couldn't refuse at her to get her to stop with the threats and blackmail. He didn't even blink an eye when he signed the check essentially buying my son for me.

I'll never be able to repay him for the money or the love he's shown both of us. I push open the SUV door and climb out.

"Tell me she signed? That mug of yours isn't screaming success. If that drug-addicted whore didn't sign off, I'll…"

"No, man. She signed everything and didn't even look back once at him. It's over. Tanner's home and we don't have to worry about her again."

Jude clasps my shoulder. "Then why no celebration? You can't be feeling guilty. Justine would have milked you dry for years if we didn't finally pay her off. Tanner's better off without her messing up his life. She's never even tried to spend time with him. She only ever shows up for threats and a payoff."

I nod. I have no guilt at all about making sure that woman can never hurt my son. It's a different type of guilt that I carry.

"It's not about her. It's Savy. Something happened, I…we…saw her. She knows about Tanner and she didn't take it well."

Jude's brow furrows. "Okay, define didn't take it well. Savy wouldn't…"

Both of our phones chime out seconds apart, cutting him off. His frown deepens as we reach for them. That chime is a special notification for a Google alert. We set them up years ago so we could keep up with what was being reported about Savy's life by the press. Jude beats me to his phone and swipes it open and then all the blood drains from his face as he looks back up at me.

"We gotta go. We gotta go, right fucking now!"

SAVY

I make it to the SUV but as soon as Patrick closes the door behind me, I break. I hunch over with my hands pressed to my mouth as choked sobs pour out. It's too much. It's all too much. Jude and Tate. Celeste trying to take Mark from me. The beautiful little boy that should have been mine and now knowing that Beck found someone else to love. It just tears me apart, shredding my barely healed heart. I have no right, no right at all to feel anything about Beck. Of course, he moved on! It's been years and I was nothing but a dumb girl he messed around with for a little while.

I tried, I tried so fucking hard to pack it all away behind the wall I crafted to keep the pain back but today is just too fucking much and it rushes through swamping me.

"Miss Sevan? Savanna?"

I gasp in a breath like a drowning victim, remembering that there's a witness to what I'm doing, and manage to breathe out the word, "Home."

I close my eyes and pull, pull so fucking hard to jam all of these emotions back inside locking them away again so I can repair my mask. I swipe the tears away, jam a pair of sunglasses on my face, and lean back into my seat with a cautious breath.

"I'm sorry, Patrick. Had a moment there but it's all good now."

I catch him looking at me in the rear-view mirror so I tug my lips enough to pass off a smile and his eyes crinkle in the corners.

"I'm sure I don't know what you mean, Miss. Traffic is heavy right now but I should have you home within twenty minutes."

I nod slowly until he looks away, incredibly grateful for his discretion. I need to clear my head so I pull my phone out to read emails and see a notification from Sara that she's taken Mo to the park. Stupid tears burn again knowing I'm headed home to an empty house. I really need someone who loves me right now and all I have is Mo.

"Patrick? Can you swing by the park instead, please? I think I'd like to go for a walk. Maybe feed the ducks."

His eyes hit the mirror again and he studies me for a few beats before replying.

"Of course, Miss. It's a lovely day to go to the park. Do you have a preference on what side you want to be dropped at?"

"Um, hold on a sec. Let me check with Sara to see where she and Mo are."

I send off a text knowing I'll never find them in the over eight hundred acres that make up Central park without a location.

When she gets back to me, I let him know they are near the Ravine so he can drop me closest to them.

I try to read emails but I know I'm fooling myself when I keep reading the same line over and over again so I shove my phone in my pocket and stare out the window leaving all the thoughts I've been trying to ignore to circle back to the forefront of my mind.

I was fine. Maybe a little lonely but fine. I had a plan for my future. I accepted that I would live it alone except for Stella and Mo and the occasional dinner with Mark. It was safer that way, easier. None of them would leave me, hurt me, break me the way a man…men could. And maybe one day if I felt strong enough, I could see about adopting a child or even getting a sperm donor. I could maybe make my own family by myself. I even managed to take care of my own sexual needs with a bevy of toys. I don't need a man for sex or love. I was doing fine on my own.

I wave Patrick off when he pulls up to the park and let him know I'll call him when I'm ready to be picked up. I walk away still absorbed in my issues.

I had put the ugly history of Celeste and Vanessa behind me. I might not ever be able to forgive them for the pain they caused me but I had stopped trying to figure out why they didn't want me, why nobody wanted to stay with me. I need to remember that. Clear all this out of disrupting my life. No more. No more Jude, no more Tate, no more anyone but me, Mo, Stella, and Mark. That's all I need. I'll get a security team if they won't listen and back off. There's nothing here or in me for them and they need to leave me alone. I can't keep circling this. It hurts too much to see them and remember what it felt like to be touched and loved. To have hope for a family of my own. I step out of the sun under the shade of the towering trees as I make my way toward where Sara said they'd be and keep working on shoring up my resolve.

I step to the right when I hear the occasional, "On your left!" as joggers and bikers pass me by but I don't see them. All I see is Jude telling me he's going to keep scaling my wall. Tate is in my office saying he loves me and then showing up in the morning just to see my face. Beck and the sweetest chubby cheeks and how I desperately wish his son to be mine, our child. These are all the thoughts I need to erase. I need to keep them out or I'll never be able to get back to the calm, steady life I had built for myself. It's too much pain for my heart to handle when…

Real physical pain grips me as my ponytail is yanked viciously to the right causing me to stumble in my heels and twist my ankle. I can't even focus on the agonizing throb of that as an arm wraps around my throat, cutting off my airway and I'm dragged off the pathway into the trees. I can smell stale nicotine coming off his arm as I thrash my arms and legs, kicking out and then trying to dig in to stop whoever has grabbed me from taking me further from the path. Dark spots start blooming in my vision as my lungs starve for air and I know I'll be unconscious any minute if I don't DO SOMETHING! I turn my fingers into claws, reach up behind me and dig into the man's face as hard as I can and drag my nails down.

I hear a grunt, a curse and then I'm dropped to the forest floor where I wheeze in as much air as I can to my starved lungs and then I roll and roll again, trying to put as much distance between me and him as I work desperately to get enough air to scream for help.

"Fucking cunt! You'll pay for that." He spits at me, drawing my wide eyes to him. He's tall, from down here he seems huge and he's wearing a baseball cap and a black face mask like we used to wear during covid that's been pulled down under his nose from my clawing. There are gouges under his dark black eyes with a trickle of blood running down to disappear into the black fabric of his mask. It's a split second to take it all in and then I pull in a lung full of air and manage a partial scream before he's on me again.

His hand swings wide and comes down hard but I tuck my chin so instead of taking it full on to the face he hits the side of my forehead. It still makes me see stars but I keep bucking my hips and shoving at him as he straddles my waist and delivers another hit to the other side of my head. My screams are coming out more like raspy cries as panic freezes my lungs but they're cut off completely when his hands wrap around my throat and squeeze.

That's when I can see it in his cold, hard eyes. He doesn't want to rob me or rape me, he wants to kill me. My hands fly out to the sides and sweep across the ground searching for anything, a branch, a rock - anything I can use as a weapon. My left hand knocks into something and my fingers tear at it to get a grip, finding a heel. It's one of my shoes that must have come off when he was dragging me. I bring it up and slap it against the side of his head over and over but it's not doing enough damage to get him to stop.

Black wings start crowding out the light from my eyes as lack of oxygen starts to take me under and my mind flashes through all the things I'll never get to have, all the things I was too scared to try for. As my arms drop down to the ground, too weak to keep fighting, I see their faces, close my eyes and I let go.

The man above me growls savagely like a wild beast, like an animal with sharp teeth that will bite and tear at my flesh and then the weight pinning me down is gone and a small trickle of air slips down my aching throat like fire. All I can hear is the ragged, sharp gaspy inhales as my lungs huff in tiny sips of air. The weight comes back and then he licks a wide path up my cheek causing a whine of terror to force itself from between my lips. A matching whine echoes back at me making my eyes fly open to meet big, warm brown ones. The cries I had been trying to force out finally break through and ring out as my heavy arms come up and wrap around the thick furry neck of my hero.

"Oh, my God! Miss Sevan? Oh God, Oh God! Savanna? Mo! Off, off! Someone call 911!"

"Chase that guy! He's getting away!"

"…need an ambulance near the Ravine in Central Park."

"Savanna, can you open your eyes?"

"Is that Savanna Sevan? Holy shit! Get a picture of that!"

"Everyone get back! Get the hell back! Can't you see she's hurt!"

I hear it all but I just hold on to Mo and keep breathing.

ASHER

"You're lucky it was a nice clean break. We'll refer you to the sports clinic and they'll set you up with a program to help get you back on the courts once that cast comes off."

I hang back as the ortho resident goes over the aftercare instructions with the teen who tried to dunk a basketball, missed, and plowed into the pole instead. I've been shadowing in the orthopedic department for a few days in a program that the team has with this hospital and I've already learned so much. I wish I could have gone through for my MD to eventually be a team doctor but facing down ten years of school, interning, and then residency - before I could even get back into sports medicine was just too much. I'm already beyond lucky that Tate pulled strings to get me on his team's training staff when I graduated. When he and Jude made their trades to the Kings, they made my job a part of the deal so we could finally all be together.

It's been good to have all of us back under the same roof and even better to have the chance to repair my friendship with Jude. Seeing Savy last week in person took a huge weight off of my shoulders even if I haven't had the courage to approach her again yet. I'm trying to stay back for now to let Jude and Tate have their time to win her back. She's resistant to all of us according to them but Jude insists he's making progress with her. When my turn finally comes along, I'm going to give it all that I have to make her see how sorry I am and that we deserve a shot together too.

"Mr. James, we're done here. Do me a favor and drop this chart off with the nurses at the central station and then come on back to our floor. I have some research papers on the rehabilitation of ACLs that I think you'll find interesting. As you know, that's a pretty common sports injury your players face."

I take the chart from him with a nod as we leave the emergency room cubicle and go in different directions. The three nurses at the station are huddled up in conversation so I wait on the other side of the counter to hand the chart over.

"Not so indifferent now, is she?"

"Ouch, Dana, you're such a bitch," one of them laughs. "Just because she's a celebrity doesn't mean she deserved that."

"I know, she's just always so stuck up with her whole attitude thing. I mean, what does she have not to smile about? She's loaded. The woman can buy whatever she needs to smile for the rest of her life. I just don't get it."

One of them notices me and holds out her hand for the chart with a flirty smile so I pass it to her and turn to walk away, not interested in hearing any of their petty gossip. I only make it a few steps away when my phone chimes out the Google alert notification for any mention of Savy in the news. I pull it from the dark blue scrubs I'm wearing as I walk to the elevators but the headline I see on the screen has me slamming to a stop.

Sevan heiress rushed to hospital after vicious park mugging.

My brain connects what the nurses were gossiping about with the headline and my feet spin me to run back. I slam a hand on the counter to get their attention.

"Savanna Sevan, is that who you were talking about? Is she here? Was she brought in?"

All three of them clam up immediately with cautious looks exchanged.

"I don't care about your gossip! Is she here? Tell me!"

One of them slowly shakes her head. "Sorry, we can't divulge that information. Patient privacy and all."

My hand on the counter clenches into a fist and whatever's on my face has all three of them taking a step back.

"She's not a fucking patient to me, she's my fucking girl," I grind out through clenched teeth. "If she's here, I need to know!"

Eyebrows pop up in surprise at that statement but one of them takes pity on me and points. "She's in bed six and, uh, sorry about what I said…"

I don't bother sticking around to hear whatever lame apology she tries to give for trash-talking a woman she doesn't know. I just race to the curtain she pointed at. My hand shakes as I reach out and gently pull it back enough for me to see Savy sitting up on the bed with a doctor checking her over. My racing heart slows slightly seeing her awake and upright even as my eyes spot the deepening bruise on the side of her face and the angry red marks around her neck. The hospital gown she's wearing covers any other injuries she might have but there's no medical team working on her so whatever happened mustn't be life-threatening.

Her hands rest in her lap and I can see the bright white of her knuckles from how tight she's holding on to them. But it's the war taking place on what I can see of her face that tells me she's barely holding on. I studied that face for two years in person and then another four through the media and I know how close she is to losing control and having her mask shatter.

She wouldn't want anyone to see that so I bark out, "She needs a minute! Get out!"

Both the doctor's and Savy's heads jerk my way, his with annoyance that quickly turns to outrage and hers that I swear has a flash of relief before her eyes squeeze closed.

"Who the hell are you? How dare you interfere with a patient's care?" The doctor snarls at me. His chest puffs up as he gets ready to blast me but I cut him off before he can start in.

My eyes never move from Savy's face when I say, "I'm the man who has loved her for the last six years and she needs a fucking minute."

The doctor sputters but Savy's soft, choked plea of, "Pl-ease" has him lifting his hands from her body and stepping back.

"Oh, um, yes, of course, Miss Sevan. I'll just see about getting you transported to our VIP floor."

He moves around the bed sending me a narrow-eyed look and then slips out and pulls the curtain tightly closed behind me. I just stand there frozen, staring at her, until she makes the tiniest cry and then I'm across the room, up on the bed, and lifting her into my lap with my arms around her. She presses her face into my neck and her knees come up like she's trying to tuck herself into the smallest ball possible to disappear entirely. I wrap her up and hold her as tight as I can without hurting her.

I bury my face in her hair and whisper, "It's okay. I've got you. You can let go now."

And she does. The sheer amount of pain I can hear in her sobs as she clutches at my chest has tears forming in my own eyes. This girl, this sweet, perfect girl is so fucking broken inside and I know it's not just from what happened to her today. I can tell from the way she's sobbing it's so much more. The pain rolling off her is years of stored heartache and it fucking kills me to know I had a hand in putting some of it there.

Eventually, her sobs calm to hitching breaths and she starts to whisper bits of what happened.

"He, he just took…me! Right off the p-path. I wasn't, wasn't s-strong enough to, to s-stop him."

I brush back her hair that's loose from someone removing her regular ponytail and try not to flinch when I feel the lump of a goose egg on her skull.

"Shh, it's okay, it's okay, sweetheart. You're safe now. It's over."

Her head shakes under my hand. "W-why? Why did he do that? W-why do bad things k-keep happening to me? What, what did I d-do?"

I brush a kiss over her hair and then tilt her chin up.

"No, no, no, angel. You didn't do anything. This isn't your fault. Nothing that's happened has been your fault. Savy, you didn't deserve this and you didn't deserve what I did to you. I'm so fucking sorry, angel."

She stiffens in my arms and tries to push off me but I tighten my arms to keep her against me. There's no fucking way I'm letting her go right now.

"I know you don't want to hear that. I know you don't want to believe me but I am. I was a fucking idiot with you. So fucking scared to love someone without bars between us that I did everything wrong. But I promise you, I'm going to do everything in my power to prove to you that I'm not that idiot anymore. Angel, I fell in love with you when you hid behind your mask and bars and then fell in love with the real you cursing like a sailor on shore leave in my house. I fucked up so bad and ruined it all. I'm going to fix it, Savy. I'll do anything if you just let me love all of you this time."

Those enchanting eyes of hers fill with more tears but she's saved from replying when the curtain is pulled back and a throat is cleared. I keep her gaze pinned to mine for a few more beats before finally lifting my eyes to the doctor hovering at the end of the bed.

"I'm sorry to interrupt, but the press is gathering so we should move Miss Sevan up to the VIP floor. It has better security and she'll be able to rest more comfortably there."

I fucking hate that I have to let her out of my arms but he's right. The ER isn't where she should be right now. I nod and gently slide Savy back onto the bed and hop down.

"Let's go."

TATE

Jude, Beck, and I step out of the elevator onto the VIP floor of the hospital with grim expressions. A security guard greets us and checks our ID against the list he holds before stepping aside to let us through. Thank fuck Ash was here or none of us would have been allowed in to see her. That was the third time we had to show our ID to even get this far. The crowd of press outside is a wake of vultures just waiting for their chance to sneak in and get the scoop on New York's youngest and most intriguing female billionaire.

When Jude tore into the house minutes after I got the alert that Savy had been attacked I had already been running for the door. Thank God, Paula distracted Tanner and waved us out so we could leave right away. We spent the drive reading what was being reported and watching the bystanders' videos of Savy being loaded into an ambulance on Twitter. She was conscious and sitting up in all the videos we saw but it wasn't until Ash sent us a message in the group chat that we all took our first breath of relief that she was going to be alright.

We tried to slip into the hospital through the parking garage but there were press camped out even down there and after Jude's picture at Savy's feet at the club opening, they connected the dots and yelled way too personal questions our way.

When the three of us step into Savy's room, her eyes lift briefly to take all of us in with a frown but she just shakes her head and looks back down into her lap. Ash is sitting in a chair next to her bed with a glare aimed her way.

"Why are you fucking glaring at her?" Jude snaps at him, earning the right to have that glare turned on him.

"Because she refuses to stay! The doctors want to keep her here overnight to monitor her but she's insisting on being discharged."

Jude strides over to the opposite side of the bed and gently tilts her head up so she has to meet his gaze.

"We gotta stop meeting like this, doll. My heart can't take seeing you hurt in a hospital bed again."

"I'm fine. It's just a few bumps and bruises and a sprained ankle," she rasps. That has me looking down at her throat and I see the swollen red and purple skin. The hoarseness of her voice with the bruising tells me that the fucker who tried to mug her also tried to choke her out. Rage rises in me that someone put their hands on her, hurt her. I want to yell at her and demand to know what the fuck she was thinking walking through that park without a security team on her ass but I push it all down and soften my expression as I step up next to Jude and reach for her hand.

"Baby girl, I'm glad you're okay but Jude's right. Seeing you in a hospital again is too fucking scary. We're going to need to wrap you in bubble wrap to make sure nothing else happens to you. Jesus, baby, this is like the fourth time you almost died."

I try to make it a bit of a joke but my throat thickens at the word died and I see Savy rear back as something I can't read flashes through her eyes.

"What? What is it?"

She grimaces as she swallows but shakes her head. "It's not your place to worry about that. It's not any of your places. I don't even know why you're all here." Her eyes dart past us to land on Beck briefly before they slide back down to her lap.

I turn my head and shoot him a pointed look. He told us on the drive what happened with Savy and Tanner earlier and he needs to straighten that shit out right now. He looks nervously at her but steps up to the end of the bed anyway.

"Savy, there's no wife. There never was. There's only ever been you, peaches."

Her brows furrow as she frowns down at her lap but when she doesn't respond, Ash leans forward into her chair.

"Tate's right. We need to keep you safe from all the crazy shit that seems to keep…" He trails off as his eyes narrow and then he's out of his chair and perching on the side of her bed with an intense look.

"Angel? I need you to tell me something. If you died, who would inherit your fortune?"

His question has me stiffening as I track back through everything that she's been through in an instant. The car accident that killed her dad and almost killed her. The strawberry champagne. Her apartment blowing up, taking out the entire floor of the building she lived in, and now this attack that might not have been a mugging at all.

Her head jerks up to meet his eyes and I see by the look in them that she's already on the same page as him but she still shakes her head.

"No, just no. He's my godfather, my dad's best friend. All of it is just a series of unfortunate accidents."

Ash cups her cheek. "But what if it's not?"

Her face crumples briefly before firming back up with a stubborn look.

"You're wrong. How would he or anyone know I was going to be in the park today? I rarely go there. Sara, Mo's dog walker, takes him there, not me. I only went today because I couldn't go home to an empty…" She cuts herself off with a quick glance at Beck. "No one knew I'd be there." She says firmly and then reaches for a cup of water. Jude beats her to it and holds the straw for her to take a sip but his expression is thunderous at what Ash has laid out.

"How did you get there? You have a driver, right? He could have told anyone where he dropped you off. Or someone could have been following you for weeks just waiting for an opportunity to get to you. This is serious shit, doll!"

I sit next to her legs on the bed and rub gently up the one closest to me.

"Alright, baby, I'll play devil's advocate. Has anything happened over the last four years? Any close calls?" She shakes her head. "So, let's say, as hard as it is to hear, that you were meant to die with your dad that day but you survived. Your inheritance went into a trust, right? So who controlled the trust before you came of age?" She makes a face and refuses to answer me so I nod glancing at the others. "Your godfather controlled it and the company, right? But just before you turned twenty-one and were going to come into full control of everything, two things happened. Your apartment blew up taking out ***your*** floor and someone slipped strawberries into your drink, both of which could have killed you."

Ash takes over asking, "What's happened recently? What's going on with work?"

She shakes her head quickly but I can see her eyes tracking through something in her mind.

"Excuse me, Miss Sevan but if you're up to it, the police are here to take your statement." A nurse says from behind us causing Savy to jerk. She looks at each one of us and then nods to the nurse.

"Can you see my visitors out please and then send the police in."

Jude growls, "Doll!"

I squeeze her leg and get to my feet. "Tell them, Savy," I say to her but am met with a blank look.

"Fuck, don't be blind to this, angel. This is your life we're talking about."

She snaps back at him and it's even worse with her hoarseness.

"Exactly! My life. Not yours, not theirs. This is my life you all barged into. Please, leave."

Ash glares down at her when he pushes to his feet but it's Jude that answers her.

"Not for fucking long, baby doll. If you think for a second we're going to fucking walk away, you're mistaken. You are our fucking life and you have been since the moment you stepped into our house all those years ago. I told you, four years, ten years, doesn't mean shit. You're ours, so get fucking used to it!"

Jude storms out past the wide-eyed nurse and the rest of us move to follow him.

I hear the nurse ask, "Do, do you want me to call security and have them removed?"

I pause at the door until Savy whispers, "What's the point? They would just find a way back even if you did."

I blow out a breath as a weight lifts from my shoulders. Now she's getting it.

SAVY

Dealing with the police is tedious with their repetitive questions asking for answers I've already given. I don't understand why they keep going in circles with the same questions when my answers never change but I try to be patient. I'm completely drained and exhausted by the time they seem satisfied that my story's not going to change and leave. The only time I even hesitated was when they asked me if I knew of any reason someone would want to harm me. I don't care what Ash and the others said, Mark would never hurt me.

I look toward the window and see that night has finally fallen on a day that seems to have gone on forever. It almost feels like weeks ago that I met with the lawyers and then had a small sweet boy in my arms. I reach out for my phone on the bedside table and wince at how everything hurts. My throat feels raw, my head throbs, my right hip aches and the side of my face is tender. I want a hot bath and half a bottle of painkillers before sliding into bed with Mo curled up next to me.

I reassure Stella one more time by text that I'm fine and let her know she can visit me tomorrow at home. I don't want her here with the press surrounding the place. I spoke to Mark briefly earlier on the phone and he's put together a statement to hopefully calm the media down. So I quickly read what he sent by email and approve it. I also asked him not to come. They put shadows of doubt in my head and I don't want to look into my godfather's eyes and question if his concern is genuine. I'm just about to text Patrick to come pick me up when the four frustrating men that have invaded my life come back in. I immediately go on the defensive when they all take seats around the bed on chairs that have been brought in.

"I'm going home. Other than some soreness, I'm fine. There's no reason for me to be here."

Jude frowns, his golden eyes filled with concern, his earlier anger nowhere in sight.

"The doctors want you watched in case of a concussion. We think you should come to stay with us."

I bark out a laugh that hurts my throat. "Hell no! We all acted out that play once before. I'm not interested in an encore or the tragic ending that will be repeated."

Ash jumps in. "Savy, even if you don't believe it, someone could be trying to hurt you. Staying alone in your house even with super-dog is dumb. You should alter your routine. Change things up so you're not predictable and you need someone to stay with you for a few days to keep an eye on that head. You took two blows to it. Concussions don't always present right away."

I squeeze my eyes closed in frustration as my head throbs and consider ringing the bell for the nurse to bring me another pain reliever. I rub gently at my temples but open my eyes when I feel something brush against my arm. Jude's leaning over me pressing the call button making me sigh in relief but I'm still not doing this. The last time I went home from a hospital with these men I ended up having my heart broken.

"Don't you have football things to do?"

Tate smiles at me like he's already getting his way.

"Nah, it's in between seasons. We do our daily conditioning but we're off for another month until summer camp starts. We have nothing to do but take care of you, baby girl."

Jude meets the nurse at the door and tells her I'm in pain and then comes back with a small paper cup with two white pills in it. I down them with a few painful sips of water as he sits next to me on the bed. He picks up my free hand and starts playing with my fingers.

"Your place, our place, doesn't matter, doll. We're sticking together until you're healed up and we know you're safe. I think we should hire a P.I. to look into your uncle."

I try to growl my frustration but it comes out more of a whine.

"It…was…a…mugging! Happens every day in this city!"

Beck's big hands come down hard on the rail at the end of the bed jolting me. He pins me with icy blue, hard eyes.

"Did he try to take your purse? Did he try to rape you? Or did he just try to kill you, Savy?"

I feel the blood drain from my face as flashes of cold, black eyes run through my mind. My body starts to shake as I remember every detail in vivid color of what happened. He never asked for my money, he didn't reach for his belt buckle or try to tear my clothes off. He just hit me and tried to strangle me. A horrible noise has me jerking back to the present and I realize the noise is coming from me. I'm off the bed and back in Ash's arms as he palms the back of my head and whispers promises that I'm okay into my hair. I slowly unclench my fingers that are fisted into claws clutching at his shirt like a life preserver and push back from his chest to meet sad jade, green eyes.

"There's not a chance in hell we're letting you out of our sight, angel. We won't lose you again."

I can feel my whole body trembling as I try to formulate an argument to make him understand that I'm not theirs to lose but before I can come up with anything someone says my name and my whole body freezes.

"Savanna? What's going on here?"

I turn my head and meet the concerned look of my uncle and sigh.

"Hi, Mark." I look back to Ash and whisper, "Can you put me back on the bed, please?"

He narrows his eyes at me and his arms tighten around me.

"No."

"Who are all of you? What are you doing in her room?" Mark asks.

Jude is quick to answer. "We're her men and this is exactly where we belong."

Mark sputters out a few half-formed sentences in shock. "Her…men, like…all of you…hers?"

Tate stands and steps between me and Mark quickly followed by Beck until there's a wall of muscle between us.

"I don't know what's going on here but I think I need to have a conversation with Savanna…alone."

Beck's voice has a menacing ring as he growls out, "No," and at almost the same time Jude says, "You're fucking out of luck there."

Mark moves across the room until he can see me and raises his brows.

"First, are you okay?" I nod tiredly at him so he goes on. "Good, you had me worried. I put out the statement you signed off on by email but the press is still out in force. Also, I brought you some things, some clothes and toiletries from your place." He looks around at the scowling men facing him and then back at me. "Speaking of the press, have you considered how…" he waves at the men in the room, "…this will play out with them? They've been salivating to pair you with a man for years but multiple men? Do you think that's wise?"

"Fuck the press and fuck you!" Jude snaps and I do the only thing I can right now. I rest my head back on Ash's chest, close my eyes and let him smooth my hair. I don't have it in me to argue or fight anymore. I'm hurting and too tired.

"It's 2023, poly's a fucking thing. Look it up! Besides, it's none of their fucking business who she's with nor is it yours."

"As long as her name is Sevan and what she does affects our brand then it is my fucking business. Who the hell are you?" Mark snaps back and I just burrow deeper into Ash's chest wishing they would all go away so I could have some peace and quiet.

"No problem. I'll marry her tomorrow and then you can keep the fucking name because she'll have mine. You want to know who I am? I'm the motherfucker that will slaughter anyone who tries to hurt my doll again. That includes you!"

I groan out, "Jude! Please! My head is killing me. Mark, thank you for checking in on me but please go away. I'll call you tomorrow and explain."

Ash leans us forward but it's just so he can snag the blanket off the bed and drape it over us. I don't catch anything else being said as the pain pills kick in and Ash's warmth takes me away.

"Sir! It's hospital policy that she leaves in a wheelchair."

"No," Beck rumbles out under my cheek and I crack an eye but quickly close it at the bright fluorescent lights flashing by.

"What's happening? What time is it?" I mumble.

I feel his lips hit the crown of my head. "We're jailbreaking you out of here, darlin'. It's four in the morning and most of the press have left for the night so we should be able to get you out unseen."

"Mmm, kay. Home?"

"You bet. Hang tight and we'll have you in a bed in no time."

My head's still achy and I know I should be fighting this, telling him to put me down and leave me alone but it's been a long time since someone's taken care of me and it just feels too damn good so I let him. I'll argue tomorrow.

"We can argue for the rest of our lives, peaches. I'll still be taking care of you." He tells me in amusement so I guess I said that out loud. I need to stop being under the influence of medication around these guys.

We come to a stop and I consider opening my eyes again but decide screw it until I hear a woman speaking.

"See if you can wake her to take these. They'll help with the transition and here's the bottle. Don't let her chase the pain, get in front of it. At least for a few days and then switch her to over-the-counter meds."

My head throbs painfully so I decide, fuck it, I'll stop doing drugs tomorrow instead and lift a hand with my palm out causing Beck to chuckle. I feel two pills drop into it so bring them to my mouth and then take the cup of water pressed into my fingers and swallow them down with a wince. I think I mumble a thank you but we're moving again and then I'm passed to a different set of arms and Jude's citrus scent envelopes me.

"I gotcha, baby doll. Go back to sleep. I've got you."

So I do, and it's the first time in years that I feel like I'm exactly where I should be.

SAVY

I open my eyes to a furry blockhead pressed against my chest and some serious doggy breath contaminating my air space. I hurt all over but I still lift my hands and dig into his fur to scratch and pet my biggest hero. I spoke briefly with Sara when the EMTs were carrying me out of the trees to the ambulance and she told me that one second Mo was walking calmly next to her and the next he was ripping his leash from her hand and galloping away. She said they weren't that far down the path from where they found me but she never heard me calling for help. Somehow, my big brute heard me and came to my rescue.

I read once that dog spelled backward is God for a good reason and I've never believed that more than I do right now as he cocks one eye open to stare back at me and a pool of drool forms on my chest. A chest covered in a t-shirt I don't recognize. I tug the collar up over my nose to get away from the doggy stink and get hit with the smell of citrus. I try to be annoyed that Jude must have undressed me to put his shirt on me but…it's fucking Jude. He's a one-man hurricane that blows wherever he wants.

I tug the shirt back down and my eyes cross when a small blue matchstick truck gripped in tiny fingers zooms in to bonk my nose. I roll my eyes to the side and see a grinning angel face looking back at me.

"Savy! You like-ed trucks?"

I look past him and see that I'm NOT in my bedroom so I sigh and say the only thing I can say in a serious tone, "I love trucks, and cars and buses and trains. I love everything with wheels."

My voice sounds like a dying frog causing the cutie to giggle.

"What's your name, handsome?"

He drives his little truck down my face over my lips and launches it off to land on Mo's big head, yelling, "Tanner!"

Mo lets out a vocal groan at the same time as one comes from the door.

"Tan-Man! We told you to wait until she woke up."

Jude moves to the bed and scoops the little boy up causing him to yell out again.

"My Savy!"

Jude sends me a wink and tells him, "Get in line, buddy. Get in line."

He swoops him through the air to the door and sets him on his feet.

"Go play. You can visit with Savy later."

Tanner yells, "Puppy!" Making me wonder if that's his only volume level and then I'm the one groaning as Mo scrambles off of me, knocking my aching body, and dives off the bed to chase after the little boy with a helicoptering tail wag.

Jude comes back to the bed and holds out two white pills. I glare at him even as I pluck one of them instead of both. I'm hurting but now that I know I'm not at home, I need my wits about me. I let my guard down last night with all of them because I was feeling vulnerable and in pain after what happened but my wall and mask are firmly back in place.

"You kidnapped me."

He passes me a water glass with a smirk.

"You bet your sweet peach ass I did. You're hurt and possibly in danger. What did you think I was going to do?"

I hand him back the glass and slide up further against the pillows.

"You could have done as I said and taken me home. You can't keep me here forever, Jude."

He climbs onto the bed to sit facing me.

"Fuck that. Forever starts right now, doll. I'm going to keep telling you this over and over until you get it through your gorgeous head. You are mine, ours, and we aren't letting you go. I love you, baby doll. I can't live another minute without you."

I shove my hands back through my hair, wincing when I touch a swollen bump.

"Why now? You had years to come for me if you really mean that. It's not like you couldn't find me! You sent enough shit to my place and my office. No, this is some kind of game to you all. You didn't believe in me four years ago and now I don't believe in you. You want to screw around? Get off? Fine, bring it on. A couple of good fucks should burn me right out of your system but everything else is off the table. You, none of you - have any say or control in my life. There is no us and there sure as hell is no forever so get that through **your** delusional head!"

He stares at me with eyes I can't read for almost a full minute, making me start chewing on my bottom lip in anxiety before a wide grin spreads across his face.

"Hmm, you're not really in any shape for me to dip my stick in your penis mitten but I can send you a penis portrait to keep you company until you are if you want. 'Course, you'd have to read my texts if I did that, right? You'd have to go alllll the way back over four years' worth of messages to catch up and find out just what game I'm really playing." He slides off the bed and gets to his feet. "With sex off the table right now, you'll just have to settle for us taking care of you instead." He walks to the door and glances back. "Tate's making you breakfast. You should come out and eat something. It'll make you feel better."

I answer him by sliding back down in the bed and turning on my side to give him my back. I hear the door close softly and blow out a breath of relief. He…they…don't get to do this, not again. They had over four years to try and fix what they broke but not one of them even tried. I'm not counting the messages, letters, gifts, and flowers they sent. If they wanted to fix what they broke, they should have fucking showed up, looked me in the eyes, and made the effort in person. Fuck their second, no, third chance!

My eyes land on my cell phone sitting on the nightstand. A cell phone full of hundreds, if not more, text messages and voicemails that I never listened to and couldn't bring myself to delete. I narrow my eyes at the damn thing and then close them so I don't have to look at it or think about what the messages might contain.

I tense when the door opens again and hear Tate say my name.

"Savy? I brought you some breakfast and coffee. Will you eat? You shouldn't take those pills on an empty stomach."

When I don't respond, he sighs and I hear him set something down on the other bedside table and then leave. As soon as the door closes, I sit up and scootch over to reach for the plate. He's made me two poached eggs, toast and a small bowl of fresh fruit and my belly growls in want as the last meal I had was lunch the day before.

As I eat and drink my coffee, swallowing it painfully, I look over the room I'm in. It's clearly a guest room, decorated in neutral décor with no personal touches in it. I'm a little surprised that Jude didn't follow his standard playbook and put me in his bed. I roll my eyes at the thought that maybe he has grown up a little bit and heard what I said by at least giving me my own space here. Then again maybe not. I'm here instead of my own home.

There are three doors and a set of glass French doors that I assume leads to the outside. I already know which door leads to the rest of the house so I slowly get out of bed, stretching my sore body carefully as I go but a small yelp of pain pops out of my mouth when I try to stand up. I look down and see my right ankle is swollen and wrapped up in a tensor bandage. I hobble-hop my way to the first door and find a closet. I sigh my annoyance at finding some of my clothes hanging in it, remembering that Mark had said he brought me some things at the hospital. The next door is a bathroom with a separate shower and a large soaker tub. My toiletries are all lined up on the counter but I'm struck by my reflection in the mirror.

There's a dark bruise on one side of my face near my temple and my hands start to shake when I remember that first blow from my attacker. My hair is a wild mess around my head and I spot a few crushed leaf pieces in it from rolling around on the ground with him. There's a dark smudge along my jawline that looks like a bruise but on closer inspection turns out to be dirt. What really has my legs going shaky and weak is the marks around my throat. I can make out a few distinct finger-shaped bruises and my eyes burn with tears at just how close I came to dying at his hands.

I suck in a jagged breath trying to head off the sob forming in my throat and turn away from the mirror. I can't let myself think about what could have happened. I'm alive and I need to focus on that so I get the bathtub filling and go back out to snag my robe and some comfortable clothes from the closet and then lock the bathroom door behind me.

I sink under the hot water and lay back to let the heat ease the aches away. I try to keep my mind blank but everything that's happened over the last week since they showed back up in my life circles round and round. Being at odds with Mark at work and now having dark thoughts about him maybe being responsible for the close calls I've had sickens me. After my dad died, he did everything he could to support me. I used to wish he would have taken me to live with him instead of leaving me in Celeste's care. I asked him once a few years ago why he didn't and he told me that the lawyers advised him against it. He was a young, single bachelor that was in control of my dad's estate and Celeste threatened to make waves if he tried to take me. It wasn't that she wanted me, I was the only way she'd be able to keep the money flowing. Now, I'm questioning all his motives and if he also didn't want me but the money.

This time I can't keep the sob from breaking free when I realize that maybe I don't have any family left at all. I draw my knees up to my chest in the water and let the tears flow. I'm so fucking tired. I'm tired of being alone. Tired of working so damn hard to keep everyone at arm's length so they can't hurt me, leave me. I just want to go to sleep and never wake up again.

The bathroom door's lock pops out and Tate rushes in with a worried frown and a bent paperclip in his hand. His face softens when he sees me in the tub all curled up crying.

"Ah, baby, I'm so sorry. Please don't cry."

I turn my head away to face the tiles and croak out, "I locked that door for a reason. I want to be alone."

"Sorry. We've gotten pretty slick with a paperclip to pop those locks. Tanner locks himself in a room at least once a week." He kneels down next to the tub and pushes my wet hair back from my face. "And I think you've spent way too much time alone already, baby girl. Some of that's our fault. Some of that's a bad hand dealt to you. Can you just let me, us, take care of you right now? Can you just lean a little bit on us, baby? Please, Savy?"

I can't force the no I know I should say out, so I just lay my head down on my crossed arms over my knees and say nothing at all. Tate must take that as consent because he grabs the bottle of shampoo off of the counter and starts softly washing my hair. His fingers are strong but gentle at the same time as he works the suds into a lather, careful not to press too hard on the bump and bruise on my scalp.

"You know I had a pretty shitty dad growing up. He didn't treat my mom all that great. He expected her to do everything for him without appreciating her or ever saying thank you. He wasn't the best role model for how to treat a woman. Lean back so I can rinse this out."

He reaches around to turn on the handheld shower attachment and set the temperature of the water. When I tighten my arms around my knees, he lifts my chin so I have to look at him.

"Not the first time I've seen you in a bath, baby girl, but I promise I won't look."

The reassurance in his eyes has me loosening up enough to tip my head back. He rinses the soap from my hair and then grabs the conditioner to massage through my hair. I close my eyes when a soapy cloth slides over my back and arms.

"When we met, I was a lot like him. I was immature, entitled, and a bit of a bully. Everything came pretty easy to me before that. Football, girls, popularity, I didn't have to try for any of it so I just expected to get whatever I wanted. You were the first person to not want me, not give me what I wanted and it made me an even bigger jerk to you. By the time I realized I wanted you, wanted you like I had never wanted anyone before, you had told me to fuck off the first time. That's when I started to change, to try to be a better person. You gave me a second chance and I felt like I had hit the jackpot but I was still learning to be a better person so even though I fell in love with you, I still fucked up. I let myself doubt you. I believed the lies Vanessa added to some truths about you. I fell back on being that entitled prick."

He gently pries one of my arms away from my knees and runs the soapy cloth over it.

"How dare she not tell me her real name? How dare she keep her job as the Butterfly from me? She's just like the other women playing games, working an angle to get with me. I felt betrayed when I had no right to be. It took all of five minutes for Jude to force the truth from her and set us straight but it was five minutes too long and we lost you."

He turns me in the big tub and washes my other arm and I can't help but peek at his face. His expression is filled with so much sadness and regret that tears slip from the corner of my eyes.

"That was the worst day of my life, baby girl. Knowing that I had the best thing that would ever happen to me in my grasp and being too stupid to keep it. I knew that guy didn't deserve you so I've been working every day since to change into the man that would."

He lifts my hand and puts the washcloth in it, meeting my eyes with his pleading ones.

"Please, Savy, just give me a chance to show you that man. Be brave, and you'll never have to be alone again."

He gets to his feet and with one last look goes to leave me to finish my bath. I whisper his name just as he reaches the door causing him to glance back.

"I was there."

His brow furrows in confusion.

"The day you stepped out on the field for the first time as a pro player. I was there in the stands and I was so damn proud of you. You weren't alone."

A range of emotions washes over his face before settling on something that makes me think maybe I should have kept that to myself. He looks back at me with hope and then gently closes the door, leaving me alone.

SAVY

They leave me alone for the rest of the day and it's a relief. Everything Tate said hit hard and resonated with me and I'm feeling conflicted and overwhelmed. I know firsthand how your upbringing can mold a person. Both of my parents dying when I was so young made me shy away from the world, hiding from letting anyone else get too close so they couldn't leave me too. Four years ago, these men started to change all that. I let myself fall for them, to care, and then ran away the minute they let me down. Most of what happened that night was their fault but I'm starting to see that everything that came after, ignoring their messages, letters, and gifts was me being scared and wanting to punish them for letting me down. I'm not ready to face my part in that so instead, I use the day to reach out to others. I start by calling my assistant.

"What do you mean Mark cleared my schedule?" I demand in annoyance.

Work is the one thing I can count on to keep my head free of everything I don't want to face.

"I'm sorry. Mr. Hanson had me reschedule everything for the next week. He said you would be out of the office recovering. Can I just say how incredibly sorry I am that happened to you, Miss Sevan? Everyone in the office is thinking of you and praying for a speedy recovery."

"Um, thank you, Mandy. I appreciate that. I'll talk to Mark and get back to you."

I hang up and immediately call Mark. I can't take an entire week off of work!

"Savanna, sweetheart, how are you feeling?"

"I'm fine. A few bumps and bruises and a sprained ankle but that's all. I just spoke to Mandy and she told me you cleared my schedule for all of next week. That's not necessary! I'll be fine to come in on Monday."

I hear him sigh deeply over the line.

"Princess, you're not fine. You went through something horrible. You need to take the week, rest, heal, and you should reach out to your old therapist. Give yourself some time."

"I don't need time. I need to work!"

"I disagree. Savanna, you've done nothing but work yourself to the bone since you started at Sevan. You work more than I do and I'm the damn CEO!" His tone is harsh but softens when he continues. "You need a break, kiddo. You need to recover and you need to figure out what's going on with these men of yours that just came out of the blue and how you're going to present that to the world. Like it or not, you're under a microscope. I'm not judging you, princess, but four men is not the norm. There will be speculation and conjecture in the press and a lot of it will be ugly if we don't get ahead of it and present it properly. Please, Savanna, take some time to figure it out before coming back. You've been through enough. I don't want to see you hurt by small minds and tabloid trash."

I want to tell him there's nothing for the press to report on but I know that's wishful thinking on my part. The press will spin anything for clickbait so I end up agreeing to take the week. At least my bruising will have faded enough to cover with makeup by then. I look down at my ankle that's propped up on a pillow with a scowl. High heels will be out for longer than a week until it's healed.

"I'll stop by tomorrow to check on you, princess. Let me know if you need me to pick anything up for you." Mark tells me.

"Um, thank you, Mark, but I'm not staying at the house right now so don't worry about that." He starts to ask where I am but I rush out a quick goodbye and disconnect the call.

I despise the doubts I'm having about Mark. I've always trusted him completely and I hate even more that Celeste's words alluded to something sinister that I had discounted but now am forced to reconsider.

My next call is to Stella and she immediately launches in on the defensive.

"Don't be mad at me! What was I supposed to do when Jude called me from your phone and told me someone might be trying to off you? You know I've always got your back when it comes to hos over bros but this is your life we're talking about! Tucked away behind gates with four big strong men to watch over you is the smart play."

I close my eyes in exasperation and groan out, "What exactly am I supposed to NOT be mad at you for?"

Stella goes quiet on her end for a few seconds before replying cautiously.

"Um, I kinda let Jude into your house to pack you some shit and take Mo and his stuff. He said you were going to stay with them for a while."

I nod slowly while pursing my lips even though she can't see me.

"So, you basically made yourself an accessory to kidnapping. Got it."

She groans, "Ah, fuck. You didn't go willingly?"

"Pretty hard to give consent when you're stoned on hospital-grade painkillers. But I had told them all before I got loopy that I wouldn't go home with them so, yeah, kidnapped and dog-napped apparently."

"Shit, alright… You want me to come and kidnap you back? I can bring the bouncers from the club to take your men down while I help you climb out of a window."

"They…are…not…my…men, Stella!"

"Uh-huh, sure. Listen, Babes, time for some tough love. I know you keep saying that and all but let's get real for a hot minute. The five of you have been connected all along. I'll always be team Savy but for the last four years, so have they. I never pushed too hard on the subject because it was low-key stalking on their part. But now? Now that they're here and making their play? It's time to sort this shit out. It's gone on long enough. You either need to fix shit with them and live happily ever dicked after or get the closure you need to move on."

When I don't reply, she sighs in frustration. "Babes, come on, you're still hung up on them. Other than a few weeks of crying and a wardrobe update, you never did what most girls do post-breakup. You didn't cut your bangs, dye your hair or go on a drunken sex binge. You just went to work and locked yourself away. Sav, you didn't break up with them and they didn't break up with you. You all just turned whatever you had into a four-year, long-distance break. They've been groveling this whole time to get you back so either talk it out and forgive them or cut them loose for good."

I chew on my lip and rub between my eyes, hating that she's right.

"But shouldn't groveling be done in person? I mean, if they truly wanted to fix it, shouldn't at least one of them have shown up before now?"

"Maybe they had a good reason for not showing up. You won't know if you don't…talk…to…them."

I suck in a deep breath and then blow it out.

"I hate when you play therapist with me and make all the sense and shit. It's annoying."

"Uh-huh, love you too, Babes. Just know, I promise to be thera-pissed off if they fuck this up again. I'll lead the rampage against them if they hurt my best girl again."

She makes me smile for the first time today.

"Kay, love you, bye."

"Love you, bye."

She echoes back in our standard goodbye to each other and I drop my phone in my lap.

Jude finds me as evening sets in and his patience with giving me space must be at an end because, without a word, he scoops me up bridal style and carries me out of the room. I keep my eyes down and my mouth shut until he walks us into the backyard and gently lowers me into a chair at a large glass patio table. There are six place settings ready for a meal and I automatically reach for the water glass near my plate and drain it in a long drink. I've been ignoring the pain since the last pill wore off and as if he can read my mind, Jude switches my empty glass out for a full one and sets the pill bottle next to it. I fish out one instead of two again and ignore his frown. Tomorrow, I'll ask if they have any over-the-counter stuff.

"There she is. Hope you're hungry, baby girl. We've grilled up a pile of steak and chicken to go with baked potatoes and grilled veggies."

Tate smiles at me as he sets a serving tray heaped with BBQ in the center of the table. Ash and Jude come out carrying more serving dishes with the sides and then Beck steps out with his son riding on his shoulders.

"Savy! 'Inally, play now?"

He calls out with a tiny scowl but Beck lifts him off his shoulders and drops him down into a booster seat at the end of the table.

"Dinner time, bud. Savy's got some owies so she needs to rest today." He glances my way with a nervous look. "Maybe tomorrow?"

My eyes go back to his son who's looking at me with hopeful eyes so I smile at him and nod.

"Yes, I'd love to play with you tomorrow. I need to inspect all your trucks and cars. Make sure they're all working right for the next race."

He bounces in his chair with a big grin showing me his perfect little baby teeth and yells, "Race! Daddy! Savy gonna race me!"

Beck gives me a soft look of gratitude that's not necessary. I would never punish his son for what's going on between us. He starts cutting up food on Tanner's plate so I look away just as Mo barrels onto the deck and comes over to head butt me in the side. My hands automatically go to his ruff to give him love.

"And where have you been all day?" I ask him as he gives me an ecstatic doggy grin, drool and all. I look over my shoulder past the massive pool and hot tub and see a wide expanse of lawn with a tall wall in the distance. "I bet you love all this room to run around. Don't you, my big strong boy? Who's the most handsome best boy? You are, aren't you?"

I look up and find all their eyes pinned on me and a blush creeps up my neck at having them see me being silly with my dog. Jude gets a huge grin on his face but looks away with a laugh.

Feeling defensive, I snap, "What?"

He wiggles his eyebrows at me still grinning.

"Well, I think you just unlocked a new kink for me. I want to hear you say that again but slower, to me. You just made my boy parts get bigger."

I have to press my lips together hard to stop the smile and laugh that wants to form and I feel a pang in my chest. I missed Jude's brand of crazy more than I realized. I look away from him so he won't see it in my eyes and land on Ash.

He's looking back at me with narrowed eyes.

"How are you feeling? Don't say fine, Savy. Any blurred vision? Dizziness or nausea?"

His questions remind me that he was at the hospital yesterday wearing scrubs so I shake my head in answer and ask my own question.

“Do you work at the hospital?”

“No. I work for the Kings on the training staff. They have an exchange program with the hospital to shadow the ortho department and sports clinic. What about your ankle and your hip? How’s the swelling? Any sharp pains?”

All of them are looking at me now waiting for my answers and it makes me uncomfortable so I reach out to take a chicken breast from the tray to give my eyes somewhere to look that’s not at them.

“My ankle is still swollen and doesn’t like too much weight on it. My hip is fine, just a little achy and bruised.”

“That’s good. How about…”

“Let her eat, man. She hasn’t had anything since breakfast.” Tate cuts him off and turns to me. “We made you lunch but when I brought it to you, you were on the phone so I didn’t want to disturb you.”

I add a few more things to my plate, keeping my eyes down.

"Thank you, but don't worry. There's plenty of days I'm too busy for lunch so no big deal."

Talking is at a minimum as everyone digs in except for Tanner who keeps up a steady stream of chatter about what he did and saw at the park, what trucks are best to race with, blue and yellow apparently - and how he's going to go swimming later with his Uncle Dude. He has a pretty good vocabulary for such a young child even if he's still struggling with some of his consonants.

The food and plates are cleared and Paula, the nanny I'm introduced to, takes Tanner away to get cleaned up and changed into his swimsuit. I wave back at him when he waves over her shoulder at me and look at Beck.

"He's amazing, Beck. He's not shy at all with me."

A soft smile crosses his face.

"He wouldn't be, not with you. He's been hearing your name his whole life, darlin'."

That makes me frown slightly. Surely his mother didn't appreciate that. Beck must read what I'm thinking on my face because he starts shaking his head.

"She hasn't been a part of his life since he was a month old." He waits for me to respond to that but my frown just deepens so he explains.

"Tanner's birth mother and I…it was a drunk hook-up when I was in a pretty dark place. I honestly don't even remember that night. I never saw her again until she showed up a month after Tanner was born and said she didn't want him. Told me if I didn't take him, she'd drop him off at a firehall."

I can't keep the shock and disbelief off my face as I sputter out, "Just like that? She abandoned him and never looked back?"

Jude huffs out a bitter laugh.

"Oh, she looked back, alright. Every time she ran out of money, she came back to make threats about taking him away from us."

My eyes bounce from Jude to Beck in outrage.

"She can do that? She can take him even though she doesn't want him?"

A grim smile pulls Beck's lips up. "Not anymore. Yesterday when you met him? We were there for the last meeting with the lawyers and a court representative. She finally signed the papers giving up all rights to him. He's mine, ours, completely now."

I don't think about what I'm saying as the words pour out.

"I can't believe a mother would do that. I would give anything to have a…"

I cut myself off with a quick, drawn-in breath and don't finish that sentence. Instead, I try to get to my feet, balancing on one leg.

"I…I think I'd like to go to bed now. Thank you for…"

"Savy, it was my fault. They didn't come sooner because…"

"Jude! Can you help me to my room, please?" I almost beg. I can't stay here. I can't hear what Beck wants to tell me with my emotions so close to the surface. I need a minute to myself to get my feelings under control but Paula comes out with Tanner yelling for Jude to get in the pool so it's Ash who comes around the table and lifts me up in his arms, repeating what he said in the hospital the last time I broke down.

"It's okay. I got you."

I expect him to offer me a shoulder but just like Jude did, he lifts me into his arms and carries me back into the house and to my room.

"You should hear him out, Savy. Beck carries a lot of guilt on his shoulders. He needs you to listen to what he has to explain."

Ash sets me on the bed, turns and goes to a dresser, and brings back a set of silk pajamas. His large hand runs over the silky material with a frown.

"No fuzzy sleepwear with cartoons?"

I take the pajamas from him with a blank expression.

"I'm not that girl anymore, Ash. You all need to realize that."

His brow furrows as he steps closer and cups my cheek, tilting my head up so I have to meet his eyes.

"Yeah, just like you need to realize that we aren't the same dumb guys that fucked up with you. We're grown men now, angel, and we all know what we want."

His expression says that's me in no uncertain terms. I pull his hand off of me and murmur a strained, "Good night."

His hand drops to his side with a sigh and then he steps back and walks out, closing the door behind him. My fingers tighten, crushing the silk at how fucking hard all this is for me. There's too much to sort through right now. I just want to go to sleep and let it all go for now so I set the silk aside and tug my shirt up and over my head and then remove my bra. I've just picked up the pajama top to slide on when the door opens and Ash comes in again startling me into clutching it against my naked chest. He freezes as hot jade eyes sweep down over my exposed skin and then my eyes flare wide as he reaches over his shoulder with one hand and pulls his t-shirt off.

I stutter out, "A-Ash…I…"

As ink-covered muscles move toward me. Heat flares between my thighs at how fucking beautiful his body is but he only slips his shirt over my head and tugs away the silk so I can thread my arms through the sleeves. His eyes are intense as he leans over me.

"I never got to see you in my clothes, angel. I'll sleep better knowing that you're wearing me close to your heart tonight."

I suck back a small gasp and his hands move from my shoulders up to slide into my hair.

"I've waited six fucking years for this, sweetheart, but I can't wait one second longer."

I swallow hard and ask, "W-waited for what?"

His lips curve up.

"To kiss my Butterfly. To kiss you, Savy, the woman I love."

He doesn't give me any time to protest as his mouth comes down on mine and his fingers tighten around my head. It's not a passionate kiss. It's a soul-destroying one. He packs so much fucking emotion into that kiss that my head spins and my hands lock onto his forearms to keep me from falling into a hole I'll never be able to find my way out of. His tongue slides against mine as it deepens and a whimpering moan escapes me as he takes me to depths I never knew a kiss could go.

When he finally pulls back, my chest is heaving as I struggle to catch my breath. He runs a thumb over my bottom lip, following it with his gaze but when those jade eyes find mine again, the awe and love in them have tears welling up. He steps back and nods to me.

"Worth every fucking minute of the wait. Good night, angel."

I sit there long after he leaves, my world rocked to the core, and then finally curl up in the middle of the bed with Ash's shirt wrapped around me and his scent in my nose.

BECKETT

I hover across the room watching the most beautiful woman laying on her stomach playing with my son with her massive dog sleeping a few feet away. Tanner hasn't stopped giggling for the last hour as Savy built an international race track for him. She divided his cars and trucks into different groups by what nationality she thinks they look like and then gave them funny voices with accents in her croaky voice and Tanner is enraptured by it. She holds up a pickup truck with horns on the hood and holds it out to him.

"This is definitely a cowboy truck so we'll add him to the American group."

She wiggles it at him and pretends to speak for it in her version of Yosemite Sam's voice.

"Tar-nation! We're gonna give them foreign ve-hic-les a US-grade thumping in this race. Ya-hoo! There's no beating good 'ole American steel!"

Tanner takes the truck with his own, "Yahoo!" and Savy moves on to cars with badly exaggerated Italian and then French accents. I'm so fucking in love with this woman my heart literally aches. To see her playing on the floor with my son with such patience and genuine enjoyment has a hole deep inside me filling in. I so badly want her to be mine, to be Tanner's- and create the family we always should have been.

By the time they have the mountain of toys separated and ready for the first race, Paula comes in to take Tanner for his nap time. He starts to fuss but Savy sits up and snags him into her lap. She hits him with a wide-eyed serious look and tells him,

"Yes! This is the biggest race ever. We need to rest up for it so we can be ready to race our best race! You won't start without me, will you? I need to have a nap so I'm ready too."

And just like that, Tanner starts to nod his head in agreement. He grabs Savy's cheeks and plants a sloppy kiss right on her mouth and tells her in his most serious tone,

"Gotta west to be weady!"

She nods back just as seriously and hands him off to a smiling Paula. I can't take my eyes off of her as she tracks them to the door as they leave with a look so full of longing that I want to push her down and fill her womb with another child of mine, of ours. I want to give her everything she ever wanted. I want to give her ten children to love. Her gaze breaks away from the door and meets mine across the room and it all just spills out of me.

"I want him to be yours too. I can't change who gave birth to him and I wouldn't because he wouldn't be who he is if I did but you could be his mother going forward. We could be a family, darlin'."

Her summer-sky eyes immediately fill with tears and she jerks her head away so I stride across the room, stepping over toys, and kneel in front of her. Lightly, I grasp her chin to force her to meet my eyes.

"I'm a big part of why they didn't come for you sooner. His mother…she made a lot of threats to pull money from us. She's the type of woman who would cross any line to get what she wants. We knew if we were with you, she would target you too. You're a very wealthy woman, darlin', and the press follows you closely. She would have found a way to use that against you, us, for an even bigger payout. We couldn't let you be hurt by her."

She sniffs back her tears. "She wouldn't have been the first opportunistic bitch I've faced down but if that was the case, what's changed now?"

I brush my fingers over her soft cheek and wish her hair was down so I could run my fingers through the silk of it.

"There's still a concern that she'll make waves for us. Justine isn't the type that will care about the non-disclosure agreement she signed for that final check. If she thinks she can make money selling a story to the press, she probably would, lawsuit or not. But she can't take him from me now. She signed away all her rights and it was well documented by the courts that she doesn't want him. That and the team trade were all we were waiting for to come back for you. I'm sorry it took so long. Please don't blame the others for that."

Her eyes slide away from mine and fill with doubts.

"It's…a lot to take in, Beck. I don't blame you for Tanner, I never would. He's an amazing gift to the world but I can't just ignore what happened between all of us and all the years in between. You can't just snap your fingers and make us a family. I can't just hand over my heart to you, especially with Tanner. The stakes are so much higher with him in the mix. I barely made it through the last time you broke my heart. If I let myself love that child and all of this blows up again, it will kill me. I wouldn't be able to survive losing him too."

She scoots back and awkwardly gets to her feet with her sore ankle and then hobbles away but I can't let her go yet. I need to try to explain what happened so I tug her back down into my lap, wrap my arms around her waist and cup her face so I can look into those eyes that I've been seeing in my dreams for so long.

"Can I tell you what happened that night? Why my messed up brain automatically went to the darkest place even though I knew your sister was a toxic bitch?"

Savy's eyes go sad and slide away but I need her to hear me and understand so I go on.

"It was because of my…mom."

Her blues flash back to mine and fill with compassion as her hands come up to cover mine, making my heart lurch at how fucking sweet this woman is. Even after what I did to her, she still has so much love to give no matter how she tries to hide it.

"I told you about her, right? How she killed herself when I was just a kid? I knew it messed me up but I didn't realize until you walked away just how bad. I've never had a girlfriend before, and never made any kind of commitment to a woman. I realized that it was always in the back of my mind that they'd leave me too and I couldn't take a chance on that happening again. My mom, the one person who should have always put me first…picked death over me. So if she did that, how could I trust anyone else to pick me? Peaches, when that bitch said all those things about you, I flinched back hard. Sucked all the love I was feeling for you away so when you didn't pick me too, I would be able to survive. I was a coward and you paid the price for it."

I breathe out all the pain that still causes me and rest my forehead against hers.

"I don't want to be scared anymore. Having Tanner has shown me that love, real love, means you have to be braver than you've ever been before. You need to be a hero in it. That means being terrified out of your mind and doing it anyway. Please, peaches, let me be your hero?"

Savy's eyes crash closed and she makes the smallest whimper so I steal it with my lips. I put everything I've got into that kiss and then let her go to help her up, too afraid to push her any further. She presses her fingers to her lips as emotions I can't read flash through her eyes and then turns and hobbles away.

Mo rolls over, chuffs at me, and follows her out.

Jude comes in a few minutes later and sits down on the play mat with me.

"She wants him, that's clear as day."

I shoot him a look. "You were listening?"

He hits me with a smirk. "Of course I was fucking listening. I didn't think I could love her any more than I already do but hearing her play with the Tan-Man just leveled me up even higher for her." He sighs dreamily. "I can't wait to see her belly all big and round with our next child."

He's so fucking certain of it and I wish I could have a fraction of his faith that this will work out between us all.

"You really think she'll give us another shot?"

His smirk turns into a grin.

"Beck, man - my doll's got a thick as fuck wall around her heart she's been hiding behind but right now it's full of cracks that are getting bigger every moment she spends with us. Trust me, it's only a matter of time and a few more well-placed shots that will crash that fucker down."

I chuckle, "You make it sound like a war."

He nods slowly as he gets to his feet.

"That's because it is. We're in a war for her heart and our future together. Don't stop fighting now, brother."

JUDE

I find Savy in the kitchen leaning against the counter sipping from a water bottle. She's overthinking shit again so time to hit her wall in a different area. I need her feeling, not thinking, to make progress. Her eyes are wary as I walk straight up to her, grasp her around the waist, lift her onto the counter, and slide in between her legs.

"Who knew a bad cowboy accent could be so fucking sexy?"

That earns me a slight smile and a soft pink blush that I want to lick.

"Baby doll, tell me you're not in pain. Tell me you're feeling okay because I have a desperate need to lick all the pink from your pussy."

Her pupils blow out in an instant as she moans. Good enough answer for me so I slide my hands up her thighs and under the shorts she's wearing and give a small tug.

"Lift that sweet ass, doll so I can get to the good stuff."

Her fingers lock on my wrists as she gives a half-hearted shake of her head.

"You can't…not here…Tanner, the nanny!"

My knuckle is dragging against her already damp panties making her denial come out in little gasps.

"Nu-uh, they won't be out until he gets up for his nap. Give me what I want, baby, or I'll take it."

I move in and slide my mouth over the smooth column of her neck, trying to kiss away every bruise and mark on it from what that fucker did to her.

"Told you, you'll let me do all the wicked things I want to your body so let me. Let me slide my tongue into your pussy and taste your cream for me. I want to suck on your clit until you break all over my face. I want to spear my tongue up inside of you so I can feel you pulse and squeeze as you come. Give me what I want, doll."

Her hips lift the slightest bit as her head falls back to give me better access to her neck. I keep my kisses light and feathery to not hurt her injury and tug her shorts and panties down until they slide off her legs to the floor. I sweep my hands back up her body and lift her shirt over her head, leaving her just in her black lacy bra, and my dick pulses painfully at the sight of her spread out and wet on my counter waiting for me to make a meal out of her.

I must stare too long because she arches her brow and lifts her chin as if to ask what I'm waiting for. I run my tongue over my teeth with a grin. Sex is when she gets her confidence back. When she thinks she's in control again. Poor doll doesn't have a fucking clue that this is just one more way to break through to her so I drop to my knees and feast.

Her back bows as I lick through every inch of her heat and then circle her clit, pulling it between my lips to suck and bite down gently on. Her moans and cries are music to my ears as I slip two fingers deep inside of her and fuck her smoothly and steadily with them. When she gasps out a different type of noise, I look up at her body and follow her line of sight to where Tate's leaning against the doorway, devouring her with his eyes. Perfect fucking timing.

"Mmm, baby doll, look at that. Look at how hungry he is for you. You want Tate to suck on your nipples while I eat you? Two mouths on your body are always better than one, right?"

I dive back in and flick her clit fast and firmly making her call out a ragged, "Y-yes!"

My fingers keep fucking into her in a perfect rhythm as Tate joins us. He slips her bra strap to the side so it falls down her arm and licks a path over the swell of her breast, making her moan. The noise spurs him on and her bra disappears in an instant. I teasingly slow down, easing the pressure on her pussy, wanting to draw this out and enjoy the view of my brother licking and sucking Savy's tits. Her eyes drop down to mine and they're clouded with desire. She bites her bottom lip in the hottest way and lifts one thigh over my shoulder to get me back to work. My cock drips precum at how fucking perfect she is and I know I'm not going to be able to resist fucking her pussy with it for very much longer.

To remind her that she's not in control here, I grab one of Tate's hands and angle it under my chin, guiding his fingers inside of her to add to mine. She stretches beautifully for us and I have images of her taking two of our cocks at once when she cries out, "Yes! Yes, more!"

With our fingers fucking her, my tongue lashing her clit, and Tate's lips sucking her nipple deep into his mouth, she lifts a hand from behind her to grab the back of my head and jams my mouth harder against her. She bucks her hips wildly with a half scream and comes for us.

Tate slides an arm around her to help support her limp form, hitting her with a savage, moaning kiss and I lick up everything she's given us from our fingers. Tate groans in need when I suck his fingers clean but then pulls away so I can get to my feet. His eyes meet mine and he juts his head in the direction of where her room is so I send him a wink in thanks for the assist and scoop my doll off the counter into my arms and carry her away.

SAVY

Holy fuck, that was a mind-blowing orgasm. Having both of them work me at the same time fed the beast inside of me that I've kept on a leash all these years. I might be trying to keep my heart protected from them but my body and its needs are something entirely different. My core throbs with aftershocks and screams for more so when Jude lays me out on my bed, I pull him down over me and slant my lips over his to kiss the taste of me on his tongue. He pulls back, nips at my chin, and hits me with a look I don't want to see right now. I don't want to think about feelings and emotions. I want to fuck.

"I love you, baby doll."

I shake my head and roll my eyes at him.

"Why don't you get your clothes off and fuck me like you don't?"

My gut clenches when I see the quick flash of hurt rush through his eyes but it's replaced by something he's never directed my way before, anger.

"You want my cock, doll? You want me to pound it home? Want me to slay this slit of yours?" He snarls and pulls back to shed his clothes then fists his pierced cock with tattooed fingers and strokes it a few times, staring at me with burning eyes. He pulls my knees up and spreads them wide then strokes that cock down my slit to my entrance. I lift my hips in welcome and he growls angrily as he thrusts deeply.

"I fucking love you."

I cry out at the burn and stretch of his size and for the words he says. His eyes are locked on mine holding me captive with anger and intensity. And then he pulls back and slams into me again with another growl.

"I love you."

Again and again, he fucks into me while saying those words.

"I love you."

Thrust.

"I've always loved you."

Thrust.

"I will never stop loving you."

He says it and fucks into me until I'm sobbing his name and on the cusp of another orgasm. He feels me tightening around his shaft and stills deep inside of me.

He places a widened hand over my heart and whispers harshly, "I love you. Now say it back. Tell me the truth, doll - and I'll make you come."

I thrash my head to the sides and try to jerk my hips for the last bit of friction I need to crest the wave but he pushes down into me with his weight.

"Say it, Savy. Say what you trapped behind that wall of yours. Fucking say it!"

Something breaks inside of me and I scream it instead.

"I love you, Jude. I love you. I love you!"

His lips hit mine and his hips piston hard and fast pushing me over the edge but he doesn't stop. I pulse and cry into his mouth as he keeps fucking me as tears pour down my face, grinding down with every thrust against my clit, tumbling me into another orgasm. His mouth lifts from mine until we're forehead to forehead and I see the glassiness of tears covering his golden ones as he says it softly one more time while he empties inside of me.

"I love you."

And there's no way to stop my heart from echoing it.

"I love you too."

Jude rolls us to the side and holds me while I cry, stroking my face and back with gentle fingers until I calm enough to pull back and face him.

"You h-hurt me. You didn't believe in me. You knew how much she hated me and you still believed her." I whisper brokenly.

Finally saying the words that have been trapped inside and poisoning my heart since that night. His eyes crash closed briefly but when they open again, they're filled with remorse.

"Yeah, one split second of doubt changed our course. I'm so sorry, doll. There's no excuse I could ever give you to make it right. I fucked up so bad, baby. All I can do is keep promising and showing you every damn day that I will never doubt you again. Please, Savy - don't keep punishing me for it because it punishes you too. Forgive me, forgive us. Make a family with me. Marry me, baby doll."

I try to move back but he pulls me closer instead.

"You can't ask me that so quickly. It's only been a few days!"

He starts laughing and then kisses me again, hard and fast.

"Quickly? Doll, I had a ring in my drawer the night I lost you. I've been waiting four fucking years to put it on your finger!"

My eyes widen and I'm at a loss for what to say. He traces his fingers over my eyebrow, across my temple, and then down my cheek to brush at my lips like he's trying to memorize my features.

"None of this has been quick. There's over four years' worth of my heart sitting on your phone. All you have to do is read it to know I never wavered except for that one moment."

He kisses me one more time and then lets me go and rolls off the bed to pull his clothes on. Jude swipes my phone from the bedside table and hands it to me.

"Please, Doll?"

He asks softly and then leaves the room. I hold the phone against my chest. I don't read the messages but I think really hard about doing it.

I manage a quick shower before Tanner wakes up from his nap and we have our epic race. Everyone joins us to play. Each of the guys chooses their own nation of cars to drive and adds their own voice with butchered accents. It's more fun than I've had in years and my laughter feels rusty the first few times but I ignore the looks sent my way by the guys, ignore Jude's looks, and focus on the little boy I'm already half in love with. Mo decides to join in on the fun by thumping his big body down in the middle of the track but before Tanner can get upset, I turn his body into a massive speed bump and send cars soaring into the air over him. Mo takes it like a champ for a while but eventually lumbers up and over to where Ash is sitting and flops down half in his lap using his big head to butt into him until Ash starts rubbing between his ears.

I glare menacingly at my traitorous dog who's supposed to hate him and snarl at him, not thump his tail and drool all over him in ecstasy. Then again, I can't stay too mad at him. I'm supposed to hate Ash too and somehow I've ended up in his arms, wearing his t-shirt to bed and swooning over a single kiss from him.

America takes the trophy, Tanner's team of course, when Italy and Germany, Jude and Tate's teams, have a massive crash that turns into more demolition derby than race. The French team, Ash's team, is disqualified due to a swipe of Mo's tail that sends the whole team off the track. Beck ran pit crew for Tanner so he wasn't in the race and my proper British team bowed out gracefully with a stiff upper lip when the American team lapped me for the third time due to lack of quick mobility, better known as a bum ankle.

Tanner chooses pizza and ice cream to celebrate his win and by the time dinner is cleaned up and he's ushered to bed, I'm ready to go as well. It's been a long few days full of ups and downs and I need some space to think some things through. I say my goodnights and hobble to my room, shutting the door firmly behind me.

I get changed and settle into bed with my foot propped up on a pillow. It's sore from using it so much today but most of the swelling has gone down and it doesn't hurt as bad as I thought it would so it must not be too badly sprained. My hip is still a little tender when pressed on and there's a nice purple and blue baseball-sized bruise on it. The bruising on the side of my face is ugly but could have been so much worse if I had taken the blow full on. Thankfully, other than a mild headache today there haven't been any other signs of a concussion. It's the marks around my neck and soreness in my throat that are the worst of my injuries. Every time I look at myself in a mirror and see them, I'm reminded of how close I came to dying and it starts the shakes all over again.

I think the prescription painkillers are the only reason I haven't had nightmares the last two nights but I plan on not taking any more of them so I'm worried I'll be haunted by replays of the attack tonight. I've been pushing away what happened every time it pops into my head but I know I'll have to deal with it or suffer the consequences of the mental blowback of it. I put in years of therapy after the car accident when I was a girl to heal mentally from that trauma so I've been trying to utilize those skills with this latest trauma.

One of the biggest things my therapist taught me was the need to accept that some things, some events, are completely out of our control and learn to be okay with that. I can rage, scream out why me, why did this happen, over and over but I'll never have an answer that will fix it.

All of that has been thrown into question now with the theory that maybe it wasn't an accident. Maybe someone caused that car crash. Maybe someone is trying to hurt…kill me. Maybe it's someone I thought I knew, trusted, and loved. All those maybes don't scare me so much as they make me so fucking sad. It just adds to what I've struggled with my whole life. The question of, why doesn't anyone want me?

I feel tears start to burn behind my eyes again so I shut that train of thought down and try to distract myself. I scroll through my phone reading an email from the media relations department letting me know that the press has calmed down after a second statement that I'm resting comfortably and that the police have no new updates on tracking down the man who attacked me. So much for distracting myself.

I drop my phone to the bed and reach back to pull the elastic from my hair, rubbing at my scalp to ease the ache that's been forming and lay my head back with my eyes closed, trying not to think at all.

ASHER

I open her door quietly to peek in and check on her. I didn't like the way she disappeared so fast after supper and I'm worried that she's hurting, especially when she didn't take her pain pills. She's sitting up in bed with her head back against the headboard with her eyes closed and her ankle propped up on a pillow. I stand there drinking my fill of her. All her dark silky hair is down, rippling over her shoulders like a silken waterfall. My favorite hair on her was once a rainbow of curls but that wig never made me want to run my fingers through it over and over and then grip it as I kiss her senseless, the way her natural chestnut waves do. I fell in love with her curves, her moves, and her eyes when she was my Butterfly but it was the quiet bookworm, the swearing and crying caterpillar, and all the other layers of sweet Savy that showed me what love truly was.

This version of her is different again. She's more confident in some ways and harder in others but under it all, still trapped in a cage. It's a cage made from invisible bars that she made herself. That fact that I'm one of the reasons she built that cage is something I'll regret for the rest of my life. When those gorgeous blue eyes of hers flutter open and land on me, the pain and sadness in them have me closing the door behind me and moving to the end of the bed. I gently place my hands on either side of her ankle and rub softly.

There's been so much piled on this woman in the last week that I don't know where to start to try to help. Us coming into her life in force, her being attacked and the doubts about her uncle's motives must be so overwhelming. I can't help with most of it but I can try to explain some of what happened back then.

I reach into my pocket and bring out the pain pill bottle the hospital sent home for her and hold it up. Her brows furrow and she chews on her bottom lip before finally shaking her head so I set them on the dresser and grab the other bottle of non-prescription pills from my pocket and offer it. Her eyes go from it to the bottle I set on the dresser a few times until she holds her hand out to take the one in my hand.

"Sweetheart, it's okay to take the stronger ones if you're hurting," I tell her with a frown. She sighs and shakes her head.

"No, I don't need them for the pain. I, I just don't want to have nightmares but that's not the best coping method, so I'll stick to the drugstore ones, thanks."

My fingers tighten on the bottle, hating the idea that she's afraid to sleep without drugs. I turn away and get her a glass of water from her bathroom and then sit next to her on the bed while she takes a couple pills and drinks half the glass and then set them aside, next to the bed. Savy rolls her head away from me to look away. I know this means she wants to be alone but I can't stand her sadness or leaving her alone right now so I reach over and shut the light off and then stretch out beside her on the bed and pull her back to my chest wrapping an arm around her waist. She's tense in my arms but doesn't try to pull away.

I bury my face in her hair and murmur, "I won't let the nightmares in, angel."

She gradually relaxes against me with a soft resigned sigh. We lay quietly together long enough that I think she must have fallen asleep until she asks in a small sad voice, "Why are you here, Ash? We weren't together back then. You…you didn't like me, hated me at the end."

Anxiousness floods through me. Here it is. Here's my chance to finally explain and try to atone for what I did to her, to my brothers, to myself. I need to get this right because I think I'll only get one shot at it. A hundred different things, excuses I could say fly through my mind but none of them feel like enough so I dig deeper straight down to the bone and share the root of it with her.

"My…therapist…she told me something once that burned through all my bullshit, all my excuses and reasons for being the way I was back then."

"You were in therapy?" Savy asks in surprise.

"Still am, angel," I tell her with a slight smile. "She told me that if you don't heal what first hurts you, you'll bleed all over the people that come after that didn't hurt you. Angel, I bled all over you and none of it was your fault."

I maneuver her onto her back and further down the bed so she's laying flat and I can see her face by the dimming light of the window. She blinks up at me but doesn't say anything so I go on.

"Jude probably told you that we grew up in a pretty rough neighborhood. Crime and addiction powered it and my family wasn't any different. Most of my relatives including my parents were minor players in a gang. There was always shady shit going down around us growing up. People would step on your back, and cut your throat just to get ahead, including my own parents and that was just a regular Tuesday for us. Anything for the next score, the next hit, and their kids were just another resource to tap when they needed something. I learned pretty quickly at a young age to hide anything of value from my own family and how best to either dodge or minimize a fist coming my way. Jude was the only person in my whole life, until Tate and Beck, to not take anything from me or let me down."

I swallow hard at the next part, the hardest part to say to her.

"I didn't - couldn't - trust anyone except them but fuck, I wanted more than that so fucking bad. Your Butterfly was the perfect woman to have more with, to fall in love with. There you were, night after night dancing for me. So fucking beautiful, looking at me with those eyes of yours. Some nights it felt like we carried on whole conversations without ever saying a damn word. If I had a shit day, there you were making it better, your eyes telling me everything was going to be okay. Having a great day? Go see my Butterfly and tell you with my eyes how badly I wanted to celebrate it by fucking you. You were the perfect fucking woman for me because you came wrapped in bars. Safely tucked away so I never had to really trust you. I didn't have to worry about you taking anything from me or letting me down."

I run my fingers over her furrowed brow until it smooths out.

"Then you, the real you, Savy - you came into my life. I watched you almost as much as the other version of you. I watched how you were with my brothers. How you never took from them, never asked for anything in return when you gave to them and I wanted that so much for me too. But I couldn't trust you. You were too close. It would be too easy to fall for you and open myself up to you taking and letting me down like so many others had. So I was a dick to keep you at arm's length but you still found a way into my heart. That night, the night it all went wrong?"

I feel my throat thicken with emotions and pause to get them under control so I don't make a fool of myself but Savy reaches up and touches me for the first time.

She brushes her warm fingers over my lips and whispers, "Tell me," with so much sweetness and understanding that I almost break. Even with all the work I've done to make myself a better man, I'll never deserve this woman. I clear my throat, breathe deep and tell her the rest.

"That night, I wasn't there to watch the Butterfly dance. I was there to say goodbye to the girl in the cage because I was finally brave enough to pick you, the real you. I chose you that night, Savy."

Her face crumples in pain and she cries, "Vanessa!"

I brush away the tears that start trickling down her face with the back of my fingers.

"Yeah, she found the exact right trigger to pull for me to blow it all up. Here I was finally taking a chance, finally trusting and she fed into my worst fears. I was furious that you were the Butterfly. It all felt like another betrayal and then she added all the other shit to it. You were a con. You were all lies. That's all it took to steal my courage and believe the worst of you. And by the time we learned that she was the one conning us and lying…you were gone."

Savy rests a palm on my jaw and says the last thing I expect.

"God, I'm so sorry, Ash. I'm so fucking sorry I did that to you."

My mouth drops open in shock and then I'm sliding over her to fit myself between her legs bracing my hands on either side of her head.

"Don't you ever fucking say that to me. You NEVER…ever apologize to me. Fuck, angel! You didn't do anything wrong. You could never do anything to apologize for."

She gives a quick shake of her head. "No, I should have told you from the start. As soon as I saw you when Tate brought me to your house. I should have told you I was the Butterfly. I should have told all of you my real name too. It was my secrets that ruined everything. It was my lies that hurt you so bad."

I groan and drop my forehead against hers. This fucking girl. This beautiful, sweet, heart-filled girl. I'm going to love her so damn hard for the rest of my life if she'll let me so I tell her that.

"Angel, I love you. I love every version, every layer, every inch of you and your heart. Please, say you'll let me love you. Say you'll stay so I can show you who I am now, who I want to be for you."

I see her eyes widen at my words and then see her retreating from me, from this moment as her wall goes back up but I can't let her. I need her too fucking bad. If she won't hear it, I'll show her until she feels it with me. My mouth drops to hers and I taste those sweet lips for only the second time but I want so much more than just a kiss from her. I want it all. I lick between her lips begging her with my mouth to let me in. I slide my hand down her arm until I can thread my fingers into her hers and squeeze. She makes a tiny cry against my lips and then opens her mouth for me. I take full advantage and tangle my tongue with hers, stroking it, exploring her mouth until her breasts are straining up against me with every panting breath.

I rock my hardening cock against the juncture of her thighs and her hips lift to chase more friction. When she starts making small mewls of need, I almost come in my pants. So fucking long. I've waited for this with my fist being the only thing to touch my cock since she came into my life. I need her like I need air to breathe.

I drag my mouth from hers down to kiss along her jaw and beg, "Let me show you how bad I want you, angel. Please, baby, let me touch you?"

Her head tips back on a moan as I lick and kiss a path down over her bruises and drag my teeth over her collarbone after nudging her shirt aside. I keep my fingers entwined with hers and use the other hand to pull her shirt collar down further so I can leave a trail of hot wet heat over the swell of her breasts. Her free hand slides into my hair and tugs me lower to her nipple, making my cock weep. I need more, more of her. I need to see these perfect fucking breasts that I've dreamed of for so many damn years so I go the other way and push her shirt up from the bottom until it's up around her neck. I suck in a harsh breath of desire when her bare breasts are exposed to my hungry eyes. Fuck, she's so goddamn perfect. I need my hands on her so I bring our joined hands to my mouth, kiss each of her knuckles and then press her hand above her head on the pillow.

"Hope you've got nowhere to go because I'm going to need a few hours worshiping your tits, angel. I'm not lying when I say these beauties have starred in hundreds of my dreams."

There's just enough light left for me to see the red blush that flares to life on her chest at my words and it makes me dip down and lick at the heated skin. I take my time on each breast licking and sucking the underside of them, cupping and squeezing them in my hands. Rolling her rose-colored buds with first my fingers and then sucking them deep in my mouth before flicking and toying with them with my tongue. I could spend hours right here feasting on her sweetness but Savy makes it clear she wants my attention somewhere else. She brings her knees up to my sides and grinds her mound against me hard, begging me with her body.

"Please, please Ash. I ache. I need…"

So do I, baby, so do I. I release her nipple with a wet pop and reach over my head to pull my shirt off, tossing it to the side so I can feel her satiny skin against mine. I bring her other arm up to lift her shirt right off and then glide my mouth down her side but catch sight of the edge of colored ink. I know she had a tiny butterfly tattoo on her hip but this must be new. I lift up enough to turn her on her side and bite down on my lip as my fingers trace the line of fluttering butterflies from the small one on her hip to the others that get bigger as the tattoo grows up her side. All her butterflies are behind black thorny vines. I lean down and kiss each one sadly. I know what this is, I know what it means. My butterfly might have stepped out of her cage but she created a new one full of thorns to keep everyone away.

"I'm going to break you free from this, angel. I'm going to help you fly."

I promise her in a husky tone and then drag her pants and underwear down off her legs. She rolls onto her back and drags me back up her body.

"I don't want to fly. I want to burn. Burn it all away, Ash. Make me forget?"

The desperate sadness in her voice breaks my heart but for right now, I'll do anything, give her anything she wants. I reach down and push my sweats off and kick them to the end of the bed. Nothing has ever felt so fucking good as feeling all her softness against my body skin to skin. I want to explore every inch of her, taste, touch, kiss, and bite but she takes control - rolling us so I'm on my back and she's straddling me. Her hot fingers drag over my chest, mapping my pecs, stalling on the little blue butterfly over my heart, and then continue down to my abs, down to my cock. Her hair falls forward brushing against my skin and it's the most erotic feeling ever. Her fingers are whisper soft as she traces them over my straining shaft and it feels more intense than if she gripped it hard.

Savy peeks up at me and the lust in those baby blues has my dick jerking against her fingers. A small, smug smile tugs at her lips and she moves her hips forward, dragging my shaft through her soaked slit. Her teeth pull at her bottom lip as she lets out a tiny shuddering gasp of pleasure and then she begins to rock back and forth, rubbing her clit against me. I thrust up to meet her slick center and can't take my eyes off her beautiful face, mesmerized by the pleasure across it that she's taking from me. I could watch her forever.

"Need you inside me. Need you to fuck me, Ash."

She moans it and it's all I need to lift her hips and spear into her. Her heat-soaked pussy takes me all the way in like it was made for my cock but when it pulses around me like it's welcoming me home emotions boil up and choke my throat. I hold her still on my shaft as I try to get a hold of them.

"Baby…I need a m-minute."

Six fucking years. Six years I've been waiting to be right here. Inside of her, a part of her, together as one. I didn't know it would hit me this hard, matter so fucking much.

Savy leans forward to place her hands on my chest, her eyes filled with shadows I can't read.

"Stop thinking and show me, Ash. Make us burn."

Her words make me grind up even deeper into her and then her hips start to roll. She takes me over, infusing me with everything she is and I give all of me back to her. Her slick cunt squeezes my cock with every roll, every thrust. Her head falls back and

I can feel the silk of her hair sweeping over my thighs but it's not enough. I need more of her, to be deeper still inside of her so I roll us again, drag her knee high up on my side and slam into her.

"F-fuck! Yes! Again!"

She cries out and I do. I fuck her with all the pent-up love and desperation I've stored up for her even as her nails dig into my back and her eyes blaze into mine and still, I want more. I slide a hand under her ass and lift her hips and swear I can feel her womb with how deep and hard I thrust into her. Her head thrashes and she moans my name as she tightens around my cock. Sweat slicks my back at how hard I'm trying to hold back my release. She's every goddamn thing I ever wanted and the pulsing velvet grip her pussy has on my cock is excruciating in the best possible way.

I growl down at her, "Give it to me, come for me, angel. Come all over my cock!

Her pussy squeezes me so fucking tight as she comes that there's no holding back. I clench my teeth as I spill inside of her but my cock stays painfully hard even as she spasms around me again and again. I can't stop fucking her. This is what perfection feels like and I'm not ready to give it up yet. I roll us to our sides and drag her leg even higher and keep thrusting.

"I...I can't! Ash...it's too much."

She sobs so I swallow her cry with my mouth and push her, push us - higher. I attack her mouth as hard as her pussy, nothing more than a mindless beast now. I want her with a fire that burns my soul. I need to feel her come again on me. So I pull out, slide down her body and lick at her clit, lap up our mixed releases until she's shaking under me and then I flip her over, drag her ass up and slam back into her. I rut into her, latching my teeth into her shoulder and it's still not enough after how long I waited for this. One hand cups a breast and squeezes, fingers tugging and rolling her hard little nipple and the other slides around to stroke her swollen clit.

"Gonna fuck this pussy so hard you'll never forget it's mine, Butterfly. Squeeze my cock, baby, milk me dry. You're so fucking tight and wet I could stay here for days fucking this pussy. Been waiting so damn long to claim it, claim you. You're my Butterfly, my angel. Fucking come for me! Give me what's mine!" I command.

She gives me it all with a scream of my name. I rear back and pump hard and fast as she pulses around me. She is sobbing into the pillow when I finally hit home, flooding her womb with my seed as my vision goes black and all I can see is her wings.

SAVY

When I wake in the morning and reach for Ash and instead find the bed empty, my heart squeezes painfully, missing him, and I know I'm fucked. These men are taking me down, one by one, like dominoes. I can't stay here. I need to leave and put some distance and perspective between me and them. One fucking weekend and they've almost torn down the protective wall I carefully crafted to protect myself from all of this. I was a fool to think that I could just have sex with them and it would only stay physical. Every touch I allow them is steeped in emotion as they try to convince me to give them another chance. It'd be so fucking easy to tip over and fall back in love with all of them but then who would be there to pick up the pieces when it all goes wrong again? No one because there wouldn't be pieces this time, there'd only be ashes left of me. I can't survive one more person that I love leaving me let alone four…five. Beck's son is part of this too. No, I won't.

I roll out of bed, ignore the ache between my legs from what Ash and I did last night and start dragging clothes into my bag. As soon as I'm dressed with my hair up and as much of the bruising covered with makeup as I can, I sweep everything from the bathroom counter into the bag and zip it closed. I need to go home. I need to go.

I leave my room and go in search of my dog. He's with Tanner and Paula in the playroom. Tanner's laying against Mo's big body as he flips through a large board book. His sweet little voice is rambling and I realize that he's reading Mo a story. I step back quickly as my heart squeezes painfully. How am I supposed to take his new best doggy friend away from him? I can't. Mo will have to stay here, at least for now. I turn away quickly and my ankle gives a pang of pain but I ignore it and rush back to my room to grab my bag, thankful that no one else seems to be around right now. I'll slip out and wait for Patrick to come get me at the front gates.

I only make it halfway to the front door when Tate spots me. His smile dims and then disappears when he spots my bag over my shoulder and he starts shaking his head.

"Baby, don't. Please, don't leave."

I pull my eyes away from his face so I don't have to see the pain in it.

"I…I have to go. Tell the others…I have to go."

Tate groans his frustration as I make it a few more steps and then he's striding toward me snapping, "Fuck that!"

My eyes go wide when he rushes up to me and takes my bag before tossing me over his shoulder.

"Tate! Put me down!" I yell but he just slaps a hand over my ass and carries me down a different hallway I haven't been in before.

"You can't keep me here against my will, Tate!"

He chuckles humorlessly.

"I'm not. But if you're going to leave, you have to tell all of us. I'm not going to let you run away without a word again."

I crash my eyes closed in frustration. That was exactly what I was going to do. Facing all of them at once will make it nearly impossible to walk away. I hear thumping music as he pushes a door open and steps into a fully kitted home gym. Tate swings me down off his shoulder and steadies me on my feet before walking over and shutting the music off. I twist my fingers nervously as Beck drops the weight bar he was lifting back into the cradle and Jude stops the treadmill he was running on. My eyes dart around the room only slightly relieved that Ash isn't in here too as three sets of eyes pin me in place.

"She wants to leave. Caught her sneaking out with her bag." Tate tells them and then asks me, "You weren't even going to say goodbye, were you?"

I let anger push aside the guilt and snap back at him.

"No, I wasn't! I didn't ask you to bring me here. I actually told you I wouldn't come here but you ignored that so you have no right to be pissed off."

Jude sighs and scrubs his hands over his face before hitting me with a tired look.

"When are you going to stop running, doll?"

My gaze darts to Beck but he just looks resigned.

"I…I'm not running. I just need to go home. I need some space from all of yo…this."

Jude steps off the treadmill, angry with my response just as Ash walks in. He looks around at all of us and when his shoulders slump I squeeze my nails into my palms.

"You had over four fucking years of space, Savy! Enough with the games!" Tate bites out.

Well, fuck him! Fuck all of them.

"Games? I'm playing games? Fuck you! You're the ones playing games with me. Four fucking years worth! You keep talking about the messages you sent, the letters? You want me to read them all like that will fix everything but none of that will fix what happened."

There's a hard ball of pain in my chest that grows with each word as my voice gets louder and more desperate as the real reason I can't do this again breaks free.

"You didn't believe me! You didn't fucking choose me! You…you left me ALONE!"

The pain in my chest doubles me over so I wrap my arms around my stomach and hold on as tight as I can trying to keep my pieces together.

Just as my knees give out strong arms wrap around me and carry me over to the weight bench. Tate holds me in his lap as hands stroke my back and hair. I sit there feeling so empty that I can't even cry. My voice is flat and emotionless as I keep my eyes on the wall across the room.

"You left me alone. Four years and not one of you came. Not after it happened or all the time since. Why should I believe that you want me? All your words mean nothing because you didn't come when I needed you. You left me alone."

Jude hits his knees in front of me but I keep my eyes away from him. I don't want to look at his or any of their faces right now.

"Baby doll, fuck, fuck. We thought we were doing the right thing."

Ash tries to turn my chin to look at them but I pull my face away. His voice is soaked in guilt.

"It's my fault…again. They wanted to go to you, fix everything. I asked them if they were going to make you choose between them. Jude was going to play on the west coast and Tate was headed to Florida. They were going to win you back but then you'd have to choose who to be with. I was being…selfish. I hated the idea of you being with one of us but not all of us. I convinced them to wait. I'm so fucking sorry."

Jude and Tate chime in on top of each other.

"That's not your fault."

"We all agreed."

Beck rubs my back with a sigh.

"And then Tanner came to us and we worried about his mother going after you."

Tate presses his face to my hair.

"We should have just come to get you, baby girl. We could have figured everything else out after we fixed things with you. You'll never know how sorry we are for leaving you alone for so long."

They wait for me to respond but I'm still wound so tight with pain that I can't. Jude takes one of my hands and forces my fingers to open, scowls at what he finds and then kisses the angry red indents my nails made in my skin. He places my palm against his chest over his heart.

"Baby doll, I need you to look at me for a minute and then we'll…let you go."

I want to deny him, keep staring at the wall but something in his tone has my eyes finally sliding to meet his golden ones.

"You shouldn't forgive us. We don't deserve it for how many times we fucked up, how many times we hurt you. You deserve so much better than all of us. But you need to know this. There are seven billion people on this planet and out of all those people, every single one of us chooses you. We will always choose you, doll. So, you shouldn't forgive us but I'm asking you to anyway. I'm asking you to choose us. Choose us for forever. Knock that wall down, doll. Do it for yourself. Choose love and we will give it to you until the day we die. We will never leave you alone again."

He stares hard into my eyes for a few more moments and then moves back and gets to his feet nodding at Tate.

"Will you drive her home?"

Tate's arms tighten around me for a beat but then loosen and he guides me up off his lap and leads me from the room.

SAVY

The house feels barren and lonely without Mo in it but maybe that's just a reflection of what's inside of me. I can't seem to settle in one place for very long. I ghost from room to room, floor to floor - searching for something I can't name. Is this what I'm going to be faced with now? Forever alone in this big empty house with nothing but work to keep me occupied? I thought this was what I wanted. Keep everyone away at arm's length so that I couldn't be hurt again. Live my life alone so I never have to feel that kind of pain again. So why does this feel so much worse? All of the things they've said to me circle around in my head over and over again. All the apologies, all the explanations, all of the…love.

The promises they all made about a future together as a family were all I wanted from the beginning. I shake my head at my own bullshit. It's all I ever wanted, period. That's all I want now. I feel like I'm back to that sad little girl I was so long ago. Waiting for my daddy to come home to give me an hour of his precious time. Begging him not to leave me as he grew cold in that car. Wishing Celeste and Vanessa would love me so we could be a family together. Falling for four stupid boys that I thought might love me back. And now pushing the men they've grown into away so they don't let me down again.

Jude's words circle around in my head.

"Bullshit, Savy. You didn't give me everything. You gave me a fucking peek over the wall you hide behind. A small glimpse of who you really are and it made me fall head over heels in love with you."

I can't lie to myself anymore. He's right. I kept so much from them all back then. So careful to hide behind masks, bars, and walls - and they still somehow came to want me, love me. Of course shit was going to blow up in my face. I was a coward, too fucking scared to tell them everything, to share all I was with them. They made mistakes but so did I. All their words hit me.

"I'm going to break you free from this, angel. I'm going to help you fly."

"I want him to be yours too. I can't change who gave birth to him and I wouldn't because he wouldn't be who he is if I did but you could be his mother going forward. We could be a family, darlin'."

"Let me be your hero."

"Please, Savy, just give me a chance to show you that man. Be brave, and you'll never have to be alone again."

"There are seven billion people on this planet and out of all those people, every single one of us chooses you. We will always choose you."

"When are you going to stop running, doll?"

"I'm asking you to choose us. Choose us for forever. Knock that wall down, doll. Do it for yourself. Choose love and we will give it to you until the day we die. We will never leave you alone again."

"Say it, Savy. Say what you trapped behind that wall of yours. Fucking say it!"

I'm so tired of being afraid. For so long I was afraid of letting them or anyone back in but now I know that what I've been doing is a different kind of fear. I'm afraid that they truly mean what they've said. That they do choose me, want me and that's almost as terrifying. I'd have to stop hiding and drop my mask, level the walls, and show them all of me. All the broken pieces that make me up and what I'm really scared of is that the real me won't be enough. I'm more afraid that I'll be the one that lets them down. That they'll leave me because I'm just not enough. They all said they don't deserve me but maybe I don't deserve them. They promised to work every day to be the men they think I deserve so if I choose them right back shouldn't I be brave enough to do the same? Work every day to be enough, be the woman they deserve?

The house is dark by the time I finally come to terms with what I've been fighting against. and I yell it out so loud that it echoes back.

"I choose them!"

I race up the stairs to the library, drag open drawers and dump stacks of letters onto the floor with the letter my dad wrote to me at the very bottom. I blow out a breath, fold it and slide it into my pocket. I need to do this before I face the first man to leave me. I pull armfuls of books down from shelves and stack them in piles in a circle. I gather all the little gifts they've sent me over the years and add them to the mess I've created and then sit down in the middle of it all and pull out my phone, swiping it open to Jude's text messages and then scroll back to that night so long ago. I start there and do like he said, I catch up from all that I denied myself and him

It starts with apologies and explanations. Pleas for me to come back gradually change to him sharing bits of his daily life. Funny moments, challenges he faced playing with a new team and the loneliness he felt not having me and the guys with him in a strange new city. Every single text he sent me over the years ends with his love for me. It takes me hours to read through them all. I laugh at some and cry over others but each one knocks another brick from the wall around me.

Tate's texts don't take as long as he didn't send as many but they're just as heartfelt as Jude's. I switch from his texts to the letters he sent me and here I find the details of how he handled moving to his new team and the struggles he faced. What has my heart healing even more is the growth I can see from his words over the years. He wrote to me about the other players at first but that gradually changed to telling me about the other players' wives and families and how much he wished he could have that with me too.

Beck's texts break my heart all over again for him. There's so much pain in them and they end a few months after I left. He told me what happened after that in person so I know how much he struggled as well. What he did send me were gifts. Little stuffed animals, candles that smelled like vanilla and peaches, and soft, fuzzy sweaters and pajamas with crazy cartoons on them. I drag on a sweater that has dogs wearing eyeglasses and reading books and snuggle down into it.

Ash sent me nothing. No texts, no letters, no gifts but I understand why. He told me about his journey in therapy to be a different, more trusting man. He couldn't reach out to me until he felt like he was the man I deserved.

The sun is coming up when I finish the last of the love letters and messages they sent to me. I stand and stretch and then scoop up an armful of the books both Jude and Tate sent to me. Each one is filled with tiny colored flags sticking out where they highlighted and made annotations to share with me. All these books are a different type of love letter. Passages are highlighted that moved them or that they found funny. Sex scenes that Jude highlighted, starred, and put a ridiculous amount of exclamation points around.

I carry them downstairs to the kitchen dining nook and stack them on the table before making a pot of coffee and some toast. I settle into the cushioned bench seat with the sun rising at my back through the window with my coffee and food and read everything highlighted. The sun rises over the house and starts to dim again when the last book falls from my fingers, my eyelids droop and I let my head fall onto my crossed arms on the table. I dream…I dream of love.

TATE

I prowl the house hungover from getting wasted the day before after Savy left. It's the first time I've been drunk in years and the aftereffects remind me why I stopped drinking in the first place. The only people in the house not affected by Savy leaving are Tanner and the nanny. Even her dog is upset. He keeps sniffing at the front door like she's going to walk back in any moment and then flopping back down in front of it with a deep yawning sigh.

This is hell. I feel so fucking hopeless right now and I know the others do too. Beck has locked himself in the playroom with Tanner. Ash and Jude are miserable from her leaving and the hangover they're both suffering from too. I find them still sprawled out on the sectional where they passed out last night.

"This is fucking stupid!" I rant at them. "We need to just go get her. She belongs here with us."

Jude drags a tattooed hand down his face with a groan and hits me with blurry, red-rimmed eyes.

"You don't think that's what I want to do? Go scoop her up and keep her hostage until she gives in to us? We fucking tried that! We can't force her to choose us. She has to do it herself. It's up to Savy now. There's nothing else we can do."

I make a fist in the hair on top of my head and pull.

"Fuck! I can't stand the thought of her all alone at her place. What if someone tries to get to her again?" I glance over my shoulder in the direction of the front door. "She shouldn't be there alone! I'm going to take Mo back to her."

Ash finally sits up and reaches for a water bottle on the table and drains it before nodding.

"We should look into getting a security team to shadow her too. She won't believe her uncle has anything to do with what's happened but we can't rule that out. There have been too many coincidences to not take precautions." He rubs a hand over his mouth. "God, I don't know what else to do."

I nod with a frown. "Alright, get Beck out here and start reaching out to some people for recommendations of personal security companies. I'm taking Mo back to her and when I get back we need to put some kind of plan in place until she figures her shit out."

Traffic's a fucking nightmare as usual as I fight rush hour. It gives me too much time to overthink all the things I want to say to her, yell at her…beg her for. By the time I pull up in front of her place my fingers ache from gripping the wheel so fucking hard the whole way. I make myself just sit there in the SUV for twenty minutes as I calm myself down and get a hold of my raging emotions. Jude's right, it needs to be her decision. It's not enough that we choose her. She needs to choose us back.

As much as I want to go bang on her door, I don't want her to think that I'm here to pressure her so I fish my cell from the cup holder and start texting her that I'm outside with Mo. I doubt she'll read it as she hasn't read any of our fucking…

My eyes go wide as I process what I'm seeing in the text thread above the one I'm typing out. My mouth goes dry making it hard to swallow as I slowly scroll up all the messages I've sent her over the years. Every single fucking one no longer has that infuriating blue-delivered check mark next to them. They all now have the pink heart I use for her contact image instead. My heart starts to race. That pink heart means my baby girl has finally, finally read my messages to her.

I blink back the burn of tears as hope surges through me and then tap over to Jude's contact and text him.

Look at your texts to her!

I don't wait for him to get back to me, I can't wait. I need to know if this means what I think it does. I hop out, open the back door for Mo to jump down, and race him to her door. I try to be patient after ringing the doorbell but when she doesn't answer right away my fist starts banging on it. Mo's whining and pawing at the door wanting her just as bad as I do. When I finally hear the locks being disengaged, I shove my hair back, trying to smooth it down.

A sleepy-eyed Savy pulls the door open and I wince when I realize that I must have woken her up. Before she can say a thing, Mo lunges forward and jumps up against her, pushing her further back into the house. She lands on her butt with a small giggle as he tries to lick all over her face. She manages to keep him from giving her face a bath by ducking her head into his neck with another laugh.

"I missed you too, you big baby!" She tells him in amusement and then pushes him off.

He lumbers deeper into the house and I can hear him slurping water from somewhere as we stare at each other. My voice comes out a plea as I hold a hand down to her to help her up.

"Baby girl, please…"

A wide smile forms on her face as she starts to nod.

"Yes."

My outstretched hand starts to shake.

"Yes…what?"

She takes my hand in hers and says, "Yes, to it all. I choose you too, Tate."

I haul her up from the floor, cup the back of her head and slam my lips to her forehead and just hold her there for a moment with my eyes squeezed tightly closed. She said yes, she fucking said yes! The relief that she chooses me has pins and needles prickling through my arms and legs and I just need to hear it one more time.

I pull back to look into the purest blue eyes I've ever seen and demand, "Say…it…again."

Her small fingers press over my heart and her eyes go soft and sweet.

"I choose you. I love you, Tate."

And that's about all the talking I can take as a desperate need to claim her and mark her as mine fills me. I reach under her ass and lift her straight up until she wraps her legs around me. I kick the door closed behind me, desperate to take possession of her mouth.

It's hard and deep and brutal but she must be just as starved for me as I am for her because she matches me kiss for kiss, tongue for tongue, until she's tearing at my shirt. I pull back enough to let her rip it over my head and then I'm yanking her fuzzy sweater off and then the shirt under it too. My hand wraps around her ponytail and tugs her head back so that I can get at all her silky skin and down to her breasts. My tongue traces the edge of the lace covering them until I find her hard little nipple beading against it and suck her right through the lace into my mouth. She makes the sweetest fucking moans as her fingers dig into my shoulders. I want to consume this woman as much as she's consumed me for so fucking long.

I take her down to the floor, cradling her back and head to not hurt her and then lean back between her knees and drag her pants down. Her fingers burn my skin as she works to unbutton and unzip my jeans. A rasp of frustration falls out of her as she struggles to reach far enough to push them off my hips. I lean down and nip at her chin and then lick the sting away as I wiggle out of my jeans and kick them off.

I want to be deep inside of her, hard and fast - but this means too much to me so I force myself to slow the fuck down. I drag my fingers in a long sweep from her shoulders down over her breasts, across her waist and belly, down to her thighs. I love the way my touch makes her shudder underneath me and the way goosebumps rise on her skin in anticipation of what I'm going to do to her.

I push her knee up and place it against my shoulder so I can slide my lips and tongue up the inside of her thigh. I can see the glimmer of wetness clinging to her mound and need a taste of it so I swipe my knuckles through it and then bring them to my mouth to suck her sweetness off.

"Tate, touch me. Please, please, baby, I need you to touch me."

Hearing her call me baby fucking wrecks me. It means I'm finally hers and it awakens something primal in me. Mine, she's fucking mine but more importantly…I'm hers.

I move forward and trail my straining cock through her slick wet folds, making her moan. I do it again and again - taking my time to rub my head against her swollen clit and I love the pretty way she begs for my cock inside her. I pull back a bit more so I can see the head of my cock slip into her nice and slow, stretching her pussy open with every inch I feed into it. She tries so hard to rock her hips up to make me go faster and deeper but she's not in control anymore, I fucking am.

"Damn it! Fuck! Please, please, Tate? I need you to fuck me. I need it hard!"

I bite down on my lower lip not to give her what she wants. I'd love to rail this perfect cunt of hers but not this time. It's been so fucking long since I've been inside of her, been home where I belong that I'm going to take my time and make it last. I'm going to enjoy every damn second of it.

"Shh, baby girl. You made me wait so now you have to. Lay back and take what I give you. I'm gonna fuck you slow and sweet until you lose your mind."

I cup her bent knee and press it up a little higher and out to the side so I can watch my throbbing cock slide in and out of her, dripping with wetness. I do it over and over and over - slowly and smoothly and she loses her fucking mind for me. My girl begs and pleads. She thrashes her head, cries my name, and digs her nails into my forearms as I keep up that sweet torture until I start to lose my own mind and I can't take it another second.

That first hard, deep thrust has her screaming, "Yes! Fuck, yes. Again, again, again! Tate, I love you. Do it again!"

And I break. I break all control and slam back into her. My fingers on her knee and hip dig in to hold her in place as I hammer into her sweet cunt that's gripping me so fucking tight.

"My pussy, my cunt, my fucking baby girl!"

I roar as she locks tight around my shaft and starts to pulse, milking me. I spill deep inside her shuddering body as she sobs my name.

My cock is still twitching when I pull out of her and lift her hips up from the floor to my mouth. I'm so fucking hungry for this woman that I don't think I'll ever be able to get enough. I lick and suck at her clit, our combined juices dripping off my chin as I push her orgasm further. I want her to feel this down to her fucking soul so she never forgets that I own her.

When I finally let up, Savy's a boneless mess splayed out on the floor and she's the most beautiful thing I've ever laid eyes on. I gather her up and hold her against me as I stroke down her bare back and ass with her head tucked into my neck.

"Baby girl, you can't run from me ever again," I tell her softly as she trembles in my arms. "I can't promise you I won't make mistakes, that I won't fuck things up with you but I can promise to try fucking hard not to. I need you not to run if I do mess up. You need to yell at me, curse me out, fight with me but never run, never run again. Please, Savy, promise you'll stay and fight for me, fight for us?"

Her hot damp breath against my neck lifts until her gorgeous blue eyes meet mine and there's so much fucking love in them that my head spins.

"I'm going to make mistakes too. It…it will take me time to learn how to live without a mask. How to open myself to you, to all of you. So I'll promise not to run if you promise to be patient, to have faith in me, to believe in me when I do make mistakes. I promise, Tate, from now on, every day, I'll fight for us."

I cup the back of her head so our foreheads press together.

"Baby girl, that's how we choose each other every damn day for the rest of our lives."

SAVY

After staying up all night and most of the day reading their messages and letters and then having my body rocked by Tate, I decide right here on the floor is the perfect place to have a nap. He's so warm and comfy to lay on that I whine a little bit when he makes us sit up, causing him to chuckle.

"Come on, baby girl, let's find somewhere softer to move to. There are things we should talk about and if you keep wiggling your perfect naked body against me like that I'm going to lay you back out and lick every inch of you."

A smug smile tugs my lips.

"Kay, let's do that."

He laughs, kisses the side of my head, and puts those sexy abs to use by sitting us both up. Tate snags my sweater and slides it over my head and then helps me put my pants back on before quickly getting dressed himself. He scoops me up off the floor and hugs me tight.

"God, can't get enough of you, baby girl."

He murmurs into my hair and I know exactly what he means. Now that I've knocked a good portion of my wall down, all I want to do is be immersed in him, in all of them. When he finally sets me back on my feet I hear Mo whining and scratching at the back door so I take Tate's hand and lead him deeper into the house. Mo launches himself into the backyard with a deep growl and bark, making me laugh. It's been a few days since he was here to protect his territory from the birds and squirrels. I leave him to it and keep the door cracked so he can come back in when he's ready.

I find Tate standing next to the dining nook that's still piled high with all the books he and Jude had sent to me over the years. He has a hand pressed to his mouth and a sheen of tears in his eyes. There's something about seeing this large, tough man getting so emotional that has my heart swooning even more for him. I go to stand beside him and run a hand over the bristling flags that fill one of the books he sent me and look up at him.

"Thank you for sending me these. I read all your highlights and notes. Tate, thank you for not giving up on me."

He slings an arm around my shoulder to pull me closer with a huffed-out laugh.

"You have no idea how much razzing I took from the other players over all of these. I always had a book with me in between practice and games. One year for Christmas they gave me a case of highlighters and a case of post-it flags. It felt like it was the only thing I could do to stay close to you at the time. Fuck, baby girl, I missed you so much."

I reach up and cup his face.

"I…I'm so sorry that…"

I'm cut off by a harsh voice behind me that makes me go cold inside.

"You have got to be fucking kidding me!"

Tate and I whirl around in shock to find Vanessa standing just inside the back door and I blurt out, "What the hell are you doing here?"

She's still looking at Tate with a disgusted twisted expression and doesn't answer me.

"Tatum Valor, unbelievable. Clearly, you don't learn from your mistakes. What a pity. What a waste."

She shrugs one shoulder while shaking her head and then lifts a gun from her side and pulls the trigger. Everything slows right down for me as the shot rings out. I feel like I'm moving through molasses as I try to lift a hand out to him. Something wet slaps across my face as Tate staggers back, hits the table, and then slowly folds over to the floor. His hazel eyes are wide with fear as they lock onto my face and bright red blooms on his lips when he whispers,

"Baby girl…run!"

My knees fold to drop down beside him but a hand in my hair yanks me back up and shoves me against the bench seat.

"Sit the fuck down and don't move, sister!"

Vanessa spits at me and everything snaps back into place.

"What did you do? What did you do? Tate!"

I scream and make to move back to him but she jams the still-hot gun barrel against my forehead freezing me in place.

"I said, don't move!"

My hands come up slowly to show her I hear her. I want to lunge for her and slam her head against the floor for what she just did but I know she'll shoot me before I can reach her. I need to survive this somehow to get help for Tate before it's too late.

"W-what do you want? W-why, why did you shoot him?"

My voice is choked as my eyes dart from hers to the floor. All I can see is Tate's arm and I don't know if he's still alive but I have to believe he is or I'll do something stupid.

"What do I want?" She laughs bitterly and moves back a few feet. She nudges Tate with her foot and then smirks as she looks back at me. "I want what's owed to me."

She motions with her gun at me with a hard look. "Don't even think of trying anything. I'm done waiting and wasting my time on you." She glances over her shoulder to the kitchen. "You have any alcohol in here or are you still too much of a goody two shoes to drink?"

I wring my fingers together trying to come up with a plan but come up blank, too consumed with thoughts of Tate bleeding on the floor.

"Uh...um…yes, there's bottles next to the fridge in that long cupboard," I tell her.

She sends me another menacing look before turning her back and walking over to the other side of the island. I take advantage of her back being turned to scoot closer to the edge of the bench so I can see more of Tate. I bite back a cry when I take in the spreading blood underneath him and the dark wet stain on the front of his chest. His eyes are closed but I can still see the slight rise and fall of his chest giving me hope that I can still save him.

"Forget about him!" Vanessa barks as she comes back with her gun pointed my way and her free arm wrapped around four bottles of booze. She sets them on the table across from me and waves her gun. "Open them."

I reach slowly and pull a bottle of vodka my way. "Why are you doing this? Is it money? I'll transfer you as much as you want if you let me call an ambulance right now for Tate!"

Her lips pull up into an amused smirk.

"Why would I settle for that when I can have it all? I'm taking what should have been mine from the start. Did you know your dad promised to adopt me? He was going to give me his name and everything.

Then half of all this would have been mine when he died. You ruined that for me just like you ruin everything. You just had to have him take you out for your birthday, didn't you? His special, sad little Savy. It's your fault he was driving in that storm and died before he could do the paperwork on the adoption. You took everything from me! But I'm taking it back you undeserving bitch."

I open the second bottle of rum and shake my head at her.

"You think if you kill me you'll get my inheritance? Are you insane? You don't get anything. If I die it all goes to…"

"Mark." She finishes for me with an amused look and it rips painfully into my chest. "That's right. Mark gets everything and when he has an unfortunate accident in a few years, his wife will get it all."

My mouth drops open as I gape at her.

"Mark married you?"

She shrugs one shoulder carelessly.

"Not yet, but he will."

I clutch a bottle of scotch in my hands tightly as rage flares up past the betrayal I'm feeling.

"You're both in this together? You both have been trying to kill me all along?"

She scoffs, "Please! Mark's a weak little pussy boy scout. Always trying to do what's right to protect his precious little princess."

She laughs darkly as she picks up the opened bottle of vodka and starts to pour it out over all the books on the table. "It actually works in my favor that he was there that night. You remember - that booster dinner? You were never supposed to be there. You were supposed to stay the loser that you are and be in your apartment when it blew but nooo, there you were trying to be someone you're not with men you didn't deserve. If anyone started asking questions, I would have cried big fat tears and pointed to him being in town when it happened. His being such a little bitch when he saw me there too and running away just made him look even more guilty."

She sets the empty bottle down, reaches for the next one, and starts pouring it out on the cushions.

My eyes are watering from the fumes so I try to edge further away as I ask, "You did the strawberries too?"

Her face thunders as she snarls, "That fucking psychopath, Jude Dixon! I had no choice but to tell him about your epi-pen. He was going to snap my neck!"

I tug my shirt up over my nose to try to get a breath of clean air as my eyes slide down to Tate on the floor with a quick glance. I can't tell if he's still breathing or not. I have to speed this up before it's too late.

"So why now? Why wait four years to try again?"

She answers me while splashing scotch on the curtains.

"Because Mark finally grew a set of balls and stopped paying me. Told me to go ahead and release the video - that he was done being blackmailed by me. I'm going to make him…"

She turns away from me to douse the far curtains and I feel like I can finally make my move. I grab the empty vodka bottle by the neck, jump to my feet, and swing for all I'm worth at the back of her head. She's turning back towards me as it connects and shatters. Vanessa staggers to the side with a gasp and the gun still clutched in her hand goes off with a roar.

The bullet hits the marble table top and the alcohol whooshes into flames. I rear back and dive off the bench grabbing another empty bottle on my way. I trip over Tate's body and scramble back around frantically searching for Vanessa through the growing flames. All the books are on fire and within seconds the alarm is blaring out. It's connected to the security system so I know trucks will be on the way shortly.

My eyes dart from the flames to Tate, waiting for Vanessa to reappear. Seconds feel like hours when I decide I must have knocked her out and I start to reach down to drag Tate away. Just as I bend, another shot goes off and I swear I feel the bullet part my hair. I drop down, dive over Tate and grab Vanessa's leg under the table and jerk it hard as flames lick toward me. I hear her slam into the table above me and then start to scream so I scurry back out from under it and the heat that's stealing my air.

What I see when I stand back up has nausea burning up the back of my throat. Vanessa's long blond hair is a burning torch around her head as she thrashes around slamming her hands against it trying to put the fire out. She rears back and the flames from her hair touch the curtains, lighting them up too.

The gun is no longer in her hand so I reach down and drag Tate across the hardwood floor toward the front of the house. The smoke has me coughing and wheezing with every breath but I never stop pulling on him until I hit the front door. I get him out on the front stoop and fresh air, drop down beside him and press against the wound on his chest as I start screaming for someone to help. Sirens fill the night as I press harder and beg and beg and beg for him not to leave me.

BECKETT

"Fucking touchdown!"

Jude screams as I walk into the room. The ecstatic smile on his face has me stumbling to a stop. It's been years since I've seen that kind of smile on his face, not since Savy…

"What? What happened?" I ask with urgency.

Hope surges in my chest as he swings his eyes my way and his smile just grows bigger. He thrusts his cell phone at me but starts to do a hip-gyrating dance on the couch, making it impossible for me to see what he's talking about.

"Jude! What the fuck, man!"

Ash laughs when Jude dances over and shakes his ass in his face.

"She…read…my…messages!" Jude chants and then jumps down to the floor.

My hand dives into my pocket so fast I almost rip the lining out. I fumble my phone while cursing as my hands start shaking and finally get the damn thing open to the right screen. There it is…there it fucking is! All the messages I sent to her so long ago have been read. I bark out a laugh as relief fills me but then look up at Jude and Ash.

"Do you think…does this mean she wants…us?"

Ash makes a fist and knocks it against his mouth as Jude screams.

"Yeah, baby!"

Ash stands and grabs Jude's shoulder like he can calm him down.

"This is great news, Jude. It means she's thinking about it, about us but just because she finally read them doesn't mean that she's ready yet. We should wait…"

I laugh out loud at the look on Jude's face. He looks like Tanner when I tell him he has to eat his vegetables before he can have dessert.

Before he can have a full-on toddler tantrum I ask, "Tate went to see her, right? He took the dog back to her? Someone get him on the phone and ask him how she was."

Jude's eyes go comically wide and then he starts tapping out the call. He puts it on speaker so we can all hear but then groans when it goes to voicemail.

Jude calls the guy five more times back to back and then looks at us with narrowed eyes.

"That fucker! The only reason he wouldn't answer one of our calls is if his hands were occupied with something more important. Something like Savy's perfect tits! Fuck it, let's go. I'm driving!"

He swipes a set of keys from the coffee table and both Ash and I move at once to take them away. Ash puts him in a headlock and I snatch the keys from him.

"Hell no, you aren't driving you maniac! There's a reason none of us will get into a car with you behind the wheel."

He sticks his bottom lips out in a pout and I can't stop the laugh. It's so fucking good to have my best friend back.

"One four-lane change and a few pylons taken out doesn't make me a bad driver!" He whines.

I lift the keys over his head and give them a shake.

"If you behave yourself, I'll swing through Shake Shack's drive-through on the way."

Ash rolls his eyes when Jude runs to the garage door clapping his hands but he's also grinning. I toss him the keys.

"Be right there. Just going to let Paula know and look in on the little man. Make sure he's sleeping."

I stand for a few moments at Tanner's door, taking in his sleep-flushed cheeks, and let myself envision a world where Savy loves him just as much as we do. I pray that she's ready to make that happen. I step back from his door and move quickly to the garage with thoughts of the woman I love and all the brothers and sisters I want my son to have.

Jude bounces around the back seat sucking back his burgers and shake while mangling his music choice of Dove Cameron. He squeals that he could be a better boyfriend than him as Ash and I howl with laughter up front. The more we laugh the lighter I feel. It's been too fucking long since we all laughed like this. I forgot how good it could feel.

Traffic's not so sucky at this time of night and we make great time until we get a few blocks from Savy's place. There's a line of cars ahead of us that are not going anywhere due to an accident ahead. I drum my fingers on the steering wheel impatiently but the longer we sit there the more my stomach starts to sour for some reason until there's a ball of dread filling my gut. I turn to Ash and see he's got a nervous look on his face that just makes the feeling inside of me worse.

Something's wrong. I don't know how I know. I just feel it. I shove my door open and yell, "Call him again!"

I use the frame of the SUV to pull myself up to stand so I can see over all the cars in front of me and suck in a breath at what I see. There are flashing lights of emergency vehicles everywhere blocking the road a few blocks up and I know without a doubt they're there for our girl.

I drop back down in my seat and bark, "Hold on!" before cutting the wheel to the right and parking half on someone's patch of lawn and half on the sidewalk. Throwing the transmission into park and killing the engine I shout, "Let's go!"

The three of us bail out and start running. The closer we get, the stronger the smell of smoke becomes. My eyes flash in every direction as we come up to the caution tape that's been strung up but I'm not seeing what I need to see so I bust through it, ignoring the cop that starts bellowing at us as we surge ahead.

We jump over firehoses and dodge firefighters to get closer until I can see the black smoke billowing out of the door and windows of Savy's house. I'm ready to charge right fucking through that smoke when Jude shoulder checks me in a different direction. My eyes latch on to the fall of her dark waves as she battles a paramedic who keeps trying to put an oxygen mask on her. Savy pushes the guy aside again while trying to keep up with another pair of EMTs that are quickly pushing a stretcher toward the back of an ambulance. The relief at seeing her upright and moving is quickly replaced by fear when one of them shifts aside and I catch a glimpse of Tate. It only takes a split second to see the blood all over him.

I don't even know I'm falling to my knees when Ash yanks me back to my feet. Jude is reaching for Savy as he yells questions but her frantic eyes never leave Tate as they load him up and help her in beside his stretcher. Jude is manic as he grabs hold of one of the paramedics and shakes him until he says something I can't understand in my dazed state and then Jude is spinning around and charging back to us.

"Let's go! We need to get to the hospital."

Ash snags the arm of a firefighter on the way back to the car and I hear him say something about the dog being in the house and then he's shoving me into the passenger seat after digging the keys from my pocket. He drives worse than Jude to get us where we need to be as he demands answers from Jude. He passes a taxi and almost sideswipes a bus.

"What did he say? What's wrong with Tate, Jude?"

Jude bangs his head off the back of my seat with a growl.

"Fuck, fuck, fuck! He was shot! Shot in the chest. They're taking him to the same hospital Savy was in after she was attacked."

Ash slams a hand on the steering wheel as he runs a red light causing horns to blare all around us.

"What about Savy? Did you see? Was she hurt?"

"I don't fucking know, man! She was moving okay but she had blood splattered all over her face. I don't know, I don't know!"

I can't even process this. Someone shot Tate. Shot him. How could that even happen? He's okay. He'll be alright. It's Tate. It's my brother. He has to be alright.

ASHER

We arrive minutes behind the ambulance but it takes us way too long to get where we need to be. Nurses throw up roadblocks as Tate's stretcher disappears in one direction and Savy is pulled in another. They say words like privacy mandate and next of kin and they can all go fuck themselves as far as I'm concerned. Beck's a fucking shell-shocked zombie, Jude's tearing at his hair and I know he's a step away from going berserk on them if they don't let us through so I throw out a few names of administrators that I learned from the VIP floor the last time we were here and within minutes we're led back to the room Savy's in.

If Beck's a zombie, Savy's just…gone. She sits on the bed with an oxygen mask covering her mouth but her eyes are empty. The doctor and nurse keep asking her questions and getting no response. She's got blood splatter all over one side of her face and I can smell the bitter reek of smoke from the end of the bed. Jude launches right at her pushing the doctor to the side.

"Doll! Baby, I'm here, we're here. It's okay, everything's going to be okay."

Those empty eyes flicker and slowly move his way but I can tell she's not really seeing him as he grips her hand.

"Is she hurt?" I ask the doctor.

He looks from Savy to me and shakes his head with a frown.

"Some smoke inhalation but no visible injuries other than some bruising that looks a few days old. She's in shock right now so we need to closely monitor that."

I scrub at my face and nod.

"You need to get her moved up to the VIP floor. The press will be here any minute."

He looks between her and me again in confusion.

"She won't tell us her name. She won't speak at all and she didn't come in with any identification. Who is she?"

Beck seems to snap out of his shocked state at that moment because it's him who answers.

"That's Savanna Sevan and the man she was brought in with is Tatum Valor, the King's new quarterback."

The doctor's eyes go wide at hearing that and he automatically reaches for his tablet.

"I need to make some calls to notify the administration and have security alerted. Talk to her and reassure her that she's safe even if she doesn't respond. I'll be back shortly with transport to have her…"

An alarm goes off with a robotic voice calling out, "Code Blue." Cutting him off and as one, our heads turn to the rapid footsteps going past the door. The doctor shoves the tablet at the nurse and dashes for the door. With another quick look Savy's way, I follow him out with Beck on my heels. There's a crowd of people surrounding the person where all the alarms are coming from but I know it's Tate. I know it's my brother in there fighting for his life. The piercing squeal of a flat alarm tells me his heart has stopped and Beck's arm slides around my waist.

A nurse catches sight of us standing there and with an apologetic look, drags the curtain closed blocking our view. We stand there together as tears pour down my face listening to them call out and shocking his heart to try and get it going again.

I've never felt so helpless in all my life. I don't know how long it goes on until someone yells out, "Let's move him!"

And then the curtain is whisked open and we're shoved back out of the way so that they can move the bed he's on at a run. The doctor who we spoke to in Savy's room stops next to us.

"It was close but he's stabilized enough to get him up to surgery. I'll be back shortly to have Miss Sevan transported."

When we go back to Savy, we find her in Jude's lap on the bed. He rocks her, strokes her hair and back, and begs her to come back to him but she just keeps staring at nothing until her broken whisper fills the room.

"Everyone I love leaves."

JUDE

I don't give two shits about their fucking policy. I'm not letting my doll go until she comes back from the hell she's locked herself away in. Ash covers us with a blanket that I tug up over our heads as they push us through the hall to the elevator that will take us away from the madness the emergency room has descended into.

Word has gotten out that the Sevan heiress and the new star quarterback are here. The media is in a feeding frenzy and even regular people are trying to get a look or snap a picture to sell to the press. Beck and Ash are playing bouncer at the door only letting in medical staff with proper hospital IDs. Some fucker in scrubs tried to get in with a camera and started yelling about freedom of the press when the boys pushed him back out. They finally got some security on the door but through it all, my baby doll stayed checked out. Except for that one heartbreaking sentence she whispered, she hasn't spoken or looked at any of us.

I tighten my arms around her as we ride up in the elevator and do something I haven't done since I was a kid. I pray. I pray to God to not take my brother from me, from us. I don't know how any of us could survive losing him and I know that Savy won't. After all she's been through, losing her parents, losing us - and now Tate? I don't think she'll come back from that if he dies.

None of us knows what the fuck happened in that house tonight. All we know is that Tate was shot and the house was on fire and Savy's not talking. Hours roll by as we wait for news on Tate's condition. The waiting rooms fill up with the team's public relations reps, the coaching staff, and some of the other players we were just starting to get to know. Savy's uncle shows up but we bar him from her room. Until we know what went down, no one's getting close to her. If I find out he had any part of this, the cops won't have a chance to touch him. He'll never be seen again.

"Baby, baby, baby doll. Come on, I need you to come back to me. Please, Savy. Please, talk to me?"

I beg her as I wipe a warm cloth over her to clean what I now know is Tate's blood from her face. I tug her smoky-smelling sweater off and pass it to Beck to be thrown away and start wiping her chest and arms down, trying to rid her of that awful smell.

"I sent this to her."

I glance at Beck and see him holding the fuzzy cartoon-covered sweater in his hands.

"It was one of the gifts I sent her while we were apart." His sad eyes lift to mine. "She never wears anything like this anymore. It's always black. If she was wearing this, does that mean she…?"

He trails off with a deep helpless frown as Ash drops a hand on his shoulder and squeezes.

"I don't know. She read all your messages and she was wearing that so maybe she was ready to forgive us. Maybe she was ready to be ours again. I just don't know."

I turn back to Savy and keep washing her down. Ash hands me a hospital gown to put on her but Beck snatches it away and tosses it into a chair and then pulls his Henley off and the t-shirt he's wearing underneath it and passes it to me before putting his Henley back on.

"Put that on her. She needs to feel and smell us around her right now. Not some bleachy-smelling hospital rag."

I slide the shirt over her head and thread her arms through it and then pull the elastic from her wrist, gather her hair back, and put it into a low ponytail. She still smells like smoke and will until I can wash her hair but that should help a little bit.

Just as I get her settled again, the door opens and a new doctor comes in. He looks at all four of us with confusion.

"I'm Dr. Nash, I performed the surgery on Mr. Valor. Which one of you is his next of kin?"

Beck snaps, "We all are," before anyone else can respond.

The doctor's brows furrow but he starts to nod.

"Alright, he's out of surgery in the ICU in critical condition but he's stable for now. It was touch and go for a while and we lost him twice on the table. The next twenty-four hours are crucial. The good news is that he's young and in peak condition as an athlete. That will help a lot in his recovery. Barring any complications, I'm optimistic about his recovery."

Relief fills me and makes me want to cry but I have to ask, "Will he be able to play again?"

He immediately starts shaking his head causing my stomach to roll.

"I won't even speculate on that. It's way too early to even consider it. The bullet penetrated one of his lungs and did considerable damage. Right now, we need to concentrate on getting him through these next few days. Everything else is secondary to that."

Beck moves over and holds out a hand for the doctor to shake, thanking him for all he did to save our brother.

Before he leaves, he tells us, "The police are looking for a statement from Miss. Sevan on what happened but due to her condition, we've held them off for now. Has she spoken at all?"

When we all shake our heads he frowns and says, "I'm going to have someone from the psych department come up and evaluate her. Someone will be by soon."

I pull Savy back into my arms with a protective growl. I want to tell the guy to shove his evaluation but the longer she stays locked in her head, the more terrified I am that she'll never come back to me so I just nod in agreement.

SAVY

Everybody leaves. Everybody leaves. Everybody leaves…me.

"We're not leaving, angel. We'll never leave. I'm here and Jude's here and Beck's here. Tate's here too, he's alive. Look at me, Savy. I need you to come back so we can take you to see Tate. He's waiting for you. He needs you."

Tate? Tate didn't leave? No, that's not right. I saw him, I saw him leave me. I heard that horrible sound in the ambulance. That angry, shrill, drawn-out sound that meant he was gone. That I took too long. That I couldn't save him just like I couldn't save my dad. Everyone leaves and it's…always…my…fault.

"Baby doll? Fuck! She's still not hearing us. What do we do? What do we do? It's been three fucking days?"

I don't want to hear them. I wish they'd go away. I want the silence. It's easier here. It's better here where I'm alone so no one else can leave.

"…pitch a fit if they catch us!"

"Don't fucking care. We've tried everything else. She needs **him**."

My head feels spinny and weird. I can feel my body moving but I can't feel the ground under my feet. Why won't they just stop, go away?

More noises make me frown. Beeps and whooshes and whispered words I can't make out. I want the silence back. I don't want to hear anything, I don't want to feel anything. It's better to be alone…

"Baby girl? Savy baby, please wake up. I need you. I need you so bad, baby."

It's a croaked, hoarse voice saying that but it's a lie. That voice is gone. He left me.

"Savy, you said you chose me. You said you love me. You promised, baby. You promised you wouldn't r-run again. You promised to choose us every day, baby girl."

That voice, it's so raw, so b-broken. I feel wetness on my cheeks and then pain in my chest be-because I did. I did promise to choose him. I promised to choose all of them.

A shaking hand cups my cheek and I feel the warmth of it slide down my neck and fill the rest of me. I feel his warmth for the first time in I don't know how long and it tells me…he didn't leave. He didn't leave me. I let my head tilt into that warmth and blink my dry eyes a few times and then I see him. I see him and I'm not alone.

SAVY

The hospital gave us a family suite to be close to Tate, not that they won't bill me for it but money's not a concern for any of us. All that matters is Tate. The room has two deep comfortable couches and a few beds in it and apparently, we've been camped out here for days. I slick back my wet hair, grateful to finally have the acrid scent of smoke off of me, and cuddle into Ash's side while reading a text from Sara about Mo. She assures me that there are no lasting effects from the tranquilizer dart Vanessa shot him with and the vet has given him a clean bill of health. My poor puppy has had almost as much upheaval in the last week as I have.

I've given my statement to the police about what happened and now all that's left is to have a conversation I've been dreading. I breathe deeply, triggering a cough and taste smoke at the back of my throat. Ash hands me a glass of water and after a sip I nod to Beck to let him in.

Mark strides in with an angry expression but it melts away when he scans me from head to toe and it turns to a hurt look.

"Princess, I've been going out of my mind. I don't understand why you wouldn't let me in. Savanna, I'm not the enemy!"

I give him a strained smile and wave to a chair across from me for him to sit in.

"I hope that's true, Mark, but there are some things that we need to discuss. Things that won't be pleasant."

He slowly lowers himself into the chair, sending cautious glances to the men who are all glaring at him menacingly.

"I…I don't understand. They told me there was a fire and that one of your, uh, male friends was shot. Why would any of that pertain to me?"

I fidget with the hem of Jude's sweatshirt that he brought for me, trying to choose the right words, but there is no right way to explain what happened that night. Instead, all I say is one word.

"Vanessa."

I'm watching his face carefully so I see the wariness come into his eyes but that still doesn't tell me what I need to know so I go on.

"She's dead."

I catch the flash of relief in his expression before he masks it and sighs.

"But she told me about the blackmail, about the video first."

His mouth opens and closes a few times as a hint of panic crosses his face before he just looks resigned and nods.

"I'll tell you everything but can we start at the beginning? What happened that night?"

I tell him how she came into the house and shot Tate and everything she said in a monotone voice. I have to try to detach a bit from what happened or it sends me into a spiral. It's going to take time for me to come to terms with it all and stop blaming myself for putting Tate in danger. I've spoken with one of the hospital's psychiatrists a few times and have plans to start seeing my own therapist on a regular basis. Bottling up all my trauma is the reason I went catatonic for three days. Choosing them means choosing to be healthy for them so I'm going to put the work in on my mental health.

"God, Savanna, I'm so sorry that happened to you and your friend. I knew she was a horrible person but I had no idea she was that unhinged." He scrubs at his face with a weary sigh. "She was blackmailing me but I promise you I didn't do anything wrong! Vanessa drugged me, I think it's called a roofie? She slipped it into my drink when she was sixteen and once I was out of it, she stripped naked and took a video with her on my lap. I swear on your father's memory, I would never touch that girl willingly! She's been threatening to show that video to her mother and have me brought up on charges ever since. It would have been a terrible scandal if it got out. So I just gave her what she wanted. At first, it was small things. Use of the jet whenever she wanted, extra money when her mother would cut her off, and cleaning up her messes when she made them."

I hold up a finger to stop him and ask, "The girl she bullied into killing herself? Her transferring to my school?"

A chagrined look covers his face as he slowly nods.

"Yes, that was me. I convinced the board to cover it up. I'm so sorry Savanna."

I nod abruptly but look away.

"She said you stopped paying, told her to go ahead and release it."

Mark takes a deep breath and shrinks in on himself.

"I did. I know she showed it to Celeste and I know Celeste tried to tell you about it. When you wouldn't play ball, she came to me." He scrubs at his face. "The police have been to see her to speak to her about what Vanessa did. She reached out to me this morning and actually apologized for everything her daughter put us through. Celeste was horrified by all of it. She asked me to tell you that and to assure you that you'll never hear from her again."

I chew on my lip and twist my fingers but Ash clasps them and holds them still with a squeeze of support.

"Why did you decide to stop paying Vanessa?"

A small smile tugs one side of his mouth up.

"Because I was going to resign anyway. You were right about those contracts. When I stopped and took a look at the report you wanted, I saw that it was just a habit, doing things the old-school way. Your ideas are fresh and innovative. You are the future of Sevan, princess. It's time for you to take it in the direction you want it to go. Your dad would be so proud of you, sweetheart."

Tears clog my throat, making it impossible to speak. Jude's still glaring at Mark and when he sees I'm done with my questions, he launches in.

"I want everything on the table right now. She needs all her doubts cleared up to move forward. Did you have anything to do with her dad's accident?"

Mark rears back in shock. His eyes dart from me to Jude.

"What? Of course not! He was my best friend. I'd do anything to have him still here with us." His eyes land on me again full of hurt. "Did you really think that?"

All I can do is give him the tiniest shrug but Jude plows on.

"How could we not have concerns? Add it all up. She almost dies in that accident, her apartment blows up, someone put strawberries in her drink that almost killed her, and then she was attacked in the park. That's a lot of fucking coincidences, don't you think?"

Mark slides forward in his seat and reaches out a hand to me.

"Oh, sweetheart, I'm so, so sorry. I wish you had talked to me about this. I have a file three inches thick locked away I could have given you. I had that accident investigated from every angle. They took that car apart piece by piece looking for any tampering done to it."

I reach out and take his offered hand and ask, "Why?"

"Anger, grief? I wanted someone to blame. He had only married Celeste a few years before that and I was already seeing her true colors. She was the first person I thought of when I found out. But it wasn't her. Trust me, if she was going to kill him, she would have waited for him to put her and Vanessa in his will first." He squeezes my hand. "It was just a tragic accident. No one was to blame. The investigators told me that day had the highest number of crashes and fatalities in the last ten years before it happened. Black ice and a whiteout were the reasons, nothing more."

He lets my hand go with another squeeze and turns to Jude.

"I had that explosion looked into as well. The unit under Savanna's was vacant and that was the point of the leak. Now that I know Vanessa was trying to hurt her, I'll have my people take another look at things. She could have hired someone to do it."

I brush the tears from my face.

"She did or she implied that she did. She also caused my allergic reaction."

Jude curses harshly. "I should have killed that cunt four years ago!"

I send him a reassuring look and go on.

"The fire started before she could admit to the attack on me last week but it fits. She did all of this because she felt like she deserved everything I had. How ironic is it that for so long I wanted everything she had? I desperately wanted a mother and to be confident and popular like her. I'd be sad and pity her for all of it but I'll never forgive her for what she did to Tate. I know it makes me a horrible person but I…I'm glad she's…dead."

Beck slides down next to me and Jude sits on the other side of Ash to reach for me.

"It doesn't! You're the best doll I know. You could never be a bad person."

"It doesn't make you a bad person, it makes you human, darlin'"

Ash just kisses the side of my head.

I breathe out a long sigh and tell Mark, "I'm sorry I doubted you. You've always been there for me. Will you stay at Sevan for a little while longer? I don't know when I'll be back. Tate's still…"

He cuts me off with a wide smile.

"Of course, I'll stay! I'm still set on resigning but I won't go anywhere until you're ready. I love you, Savanna. I'll always be here for you."

I give him my first real smile because I'm starting to believe that not everyone leaves after all.

SAVY

After Mark leaves with a heartfelt hug, I settle back on the couch. Ash and Beck are on either side of me and Jude sits down on the coffee table directly in front of me and takes my hands. His beautiful golden eyes sweep up and down my body before settling on my face.

"Baby doll, Tate said you chose us when he was trying to get you to come back. Is that true? Are you ours?"

I squeeze his hands, glance at Ash and Beck, and nod.

"Be-before Vanessa came that night? I had figured some things out. I read all your messages, your letters. It made me finally realize that you had picked me after all. I owe you all an apology for being too scared to realize that."

Jude growls out "No!"

Ash and Beck move closer and stroke my back and hair.

"I do, Jude. You were right. I've been hiding from the world, from love for most of my life. I don't want to do that anymore. I want to be with all of you, build a life together." I turn to Beck. "I want a family with you if you'll trust me with Tanner."

Beck snatches me up onto his lap and buries his face in my hair.

"Thank you, darlin'. That makes me so fucking happy to hear."

When he finally sets me back down, I take a deep breath.

"I need you all to know that it won't be easy. I'm going to make mistakes. Sometimes it will all be too much and I'll pull back, go dark on you."

Jude cups my face and presses his forehead against mine.

"That's alright, doll. I'll go with you. I'll sit in the dark with you until you're ready and then I'll be the light to show you the way out."

I press my lips against his as my eyes fill with tears for how grateful I am that they still want me. Ash tugs me back and turns my head so I'll look at him.

"We're all going to make mistakes as we figure this out, angel. But as long as we remember that we love each other and choose each other every day, it will work out. We're gonna love you so damn hard, Butterfly, and I know you'll love us back just as hard."

There's so much to talk about on how we go forward together but right now the main focus needs to be on Tate. I'm going to go sit with him for as long as the ICU nurses will let me. Beck leaves to first deal with the team reps as Tate's agent and then goes to spend some time with Tanner and bring them back a change of clothes. Jude and Ash have to have a meeting with the team too but just before we go our separate ways, Ash holds me back and hands me a crumpled envelope.

"I found this in the pocket of the pants you were wearing that night when I went to throw them away. Thought it might be important."

My fingers pull the letter from my father to my chest and press it against my heart.

"Thank you for saving it, Ash. It's more important than you know."

He walks me to the ICU with a steadying hand on my back and leaves me in Tate's room after checking in on him. I sit beside Tate's bed and reach for his hand as he sleeps, memorizing his face and counting every breath he takes. I almost lost him. I almost lost all of them and it was my fault. His eyelids flutter and open, hitting me with those incredible hazel eyes.

"Baby girl, you came back?"

His voice is groggy and thick but I lean over him and sweep his hair back from his brow with a soft smile.

"I made a promise to you. I'll never leave again. I'm so sorry for what happened to you, Tate. It's all my fault."

He rolls his eyes at me. "Un-hun, totally your fault that bitch was a deranged lunatic. Baby, stop. You're not allowed to blame yourself for what others do."

I press his hand to my chest.

"But, Tate, what if…what if you can't play again? How can you not blame me for taking that from you?"

He yawns and shrugs a shoulder, causing pain to crumple his face but breathes through it.

"It's just a job, baby girl. It'll mean I get to spend even more time with you."

A small smirk pulls at his lips. "But if you want to make it up to me, you could play nurse and give me a sponge bath. A really thorough sponge bath."

He falls back asleep before I can tell him how much I love him with a small smile on his lips that lightens my heart.

I settle back into the chair and the crinkle of paper has me pulling my dad's letter out of my pocket. I trace my name on it and decide it is time to take another step in the healing process.

My sweetest girl,

I hope you never have to read this letter because it means I'm no longer with you and for that, I'm so sorry.

Not too long ago a colleague of mine died suddenly of a heart attack. When I went to give my condolences to his family and tell them what a great man he was, the saddest thing happened. His daughter shrugged, her eyes were completely dry and she told me she wouldn't know that because all he ever did was work.

That hit me hard, princess. It made me realize how much I've failed you. After your mother died, I lost myself in work to cope with the grief and focused all my efforts on building Sevan to ensure you would always have everything you needed in life. I now realize that I never gave you what you needed the most, time. Time with me to share all the special moments in life. I never gave you all the love and care you deserved. I shouldn't have chosen the company to build. I should have chosen you instead to build a real relationship with.

I hope if you ever read this letter it's sometime far in the future and I've rectified that mistake. Now that Celeste and Vanessa are in our lives I hope we can build a strong family so you can have all the love you deserve from not only me but your new mother and sister.

It's my greatest wish that you spend the rest of your life being loved and cherished.

If by some horrible twist of fate I'm taken from you before I can make that happen, take these next words to heart. Please, sweet girl, learn from my mistakes. Put love first, always. Sell the company or let Mark run it. Don't lose yourself to work like I did. Enjoy every moment of happiness you can grab.

Choose happiness and love, Savy. Choose you, like I should have done from the start.

You'll always be my best girl,

Love Dad

I drop the letter into my lap as tears flow down my face. I feel like my dad is in the room with me, watching over me and he knew how badly I needed to hear that. A sense of peace steals over me as I realize that I forgive him. I didn't even know I needed to, but I do. I forgive him for leaving me alone for so long even when he was alive and it makes me feel…free.

I think about his company and all I've done to work towards keeping it going and decide in that moment that I'm done. I want to live the life I **want** to live, not the one I thought I was supposed to. I never wanted to work at Sevan. I thought it was something I was obligated to do because he left it to me. I wanted to do something in literature, something that I'm passionate about and something that brings me joy. I fold the letter back up and slide it back into my pocket and pull out my phone. It's time to finally step out of the cage and tear down the wall. It's time to spread my wings and truly fly for the first time in my life. It's time to choose me.

SAVY

It's been a month since we brought Tate home from the hospital. Just as the doctor predicted, being in top physical condition helped him heal and recover at a quick rate. He still has a long way to go and his rehabilitation will take months, maybe longer, before he'll be able to throw a football again but he seems almost relieved by that. He told me last night while we snuggled in bed that all he really wants is to slow down and enjoy life and I can't argue that with what I'm about to do.

Mark steps up to my side and peeks out at the crowd before ducking back and focusing on me with a smile.

"You look beautiful, princess. I'm proud of you."

I smooth down the light blue dress that matches my eyes and fluff up my loose hair. I'm not even nervous like I usually am when dealing with the press. Maybe because this is the last step to finally being who I truly am. With a confident nod to Mark, I let the mask I've worn for so long fall away, step out into the room of flashing cameras, and give them my best smile.

I read from the prepared statement about the sale of Sevan that's being negotiated and the direction we hope it will go. I cover the bare facts of the recently closed police investigation into Vanessa's evil acts and Tate's recovery, pausing briefly before reading the standard closing statement the PR team crafted and dropping the paper to the stand. I promised myself that I would stop hiding and I'm going to stay true to that so I go way, way off script.

"There has long been speculation into my private life that I refused to address and lately there have been some outlandish theories printed about me and my love life so I'm going to set the record straight. I will not be taking any questions in regards to it and I ask that you all try to have a smidge of decency and respect our privacy." I take a deep breath and my smile gets brighter causing even more camera flashes.

"I am in love with four men and they love me back. We are in an equally committed relationship and plan to spend our lives building a family together."

Madness descends in the room as every reporter starts screaming questions but I just smile and smile and then give a little wave and walk out of the room back to my future.

Patrick drives me to Stella's place after a long day of negotiations with way too many lawyers on the sale of Sevan. After discussing it together, we decided to keep their house as our main residence. My brownstone was as good as gutted by the fire and the Greenwich estate I grew up in has too many sad and lonely memories for me to ever want to live there again.

The traffic is too much to face just to go home and change and then turn around and come back into the city so Ash, Beck, Jude, and Tate will meet me at Masks for our first official date in public and I'm so excited.

"Babes, I gotta tell you, you are my fucking hero!" Stella tells me as she drags dresses from her closet for me to try on. "I knew one day you'd step out from behind your mask and shine bright for the world to see. I'm so happy for you."

She dumps a pile of clothes on her bed and I catch a flash of sadness in her eyes before she turns back to the closet to find shoes.

"You okay, Stell? We haven't had much time to talk about you lately. What's been going on in your world?"

She waves dismissively and starts handing dresses from the pile to me.

"Same old, same old. The club is doing fantastic. It's still a lot of work shaking out the bugs but we're close to having everything run as smooth as can be and I'll be able to breathe a little easier."

I watch her closely as her smile seems just a tad brittle.

"That's great, but what about you? Are you seeing anyone? Any crazy hook-up stories for me?"

Her hand is still on the next dress but then she shakes her head with a forced laugh.

"Nah, too busy with work. I'll just live vicariously through you and all your dick-wrangling. How has all that been going and what's it like to have a kid around?"

I let her change the subject but remind myself to make time to have a girls' night soon with her.

"Honestly, terrifying! Not the sex, the sex is…wow. The sex is just wow but getting to know Beck's son has been incredible. He has such a big little personality and I'm enjoying being with him so much but I'm also so scared I'm going to make a mistake with him. I don't know how to be a parent! I never really had one of my own. I'm just trying to take it day by day and be there with him, you know?"

She takes the silver dress from my hands with a shake of her head and a soft smile.

"I think that's like eighty percent of being a parent. Just show up, be there for him and show him you love him."

I arch a brow and ask, "So what's the last twenty percent then?"

Stella grins. "Wine. At least according to my mom." She tosses a few more dresses aside and then yells, "Aha! This one! I think you're finally ready for this."

She passes me the shiny lipstick red dress with a knowing look.

"You're finally ready for red, babes."

I bite my bottom lip and hold the strapless tube of pure sin against my body. There are high slits on either side and I know my men will drool over me in it so I nod as a wide smile grows across my face.

"Red it is!"

Patrick drives us to the club and we part ways when we step inside with a hug and promises to get together soon. I walk through the crowd to the edge of the dance floor as the music thumps through my body. I look up to the VIP levels and a wicked smile pulls at my lips when I see all four of them lining the rail, looking down at me. I toss back my loose hair, blow a kiss to Tate and then send a challenging look to the others. Tate still has to take it easy but he insisted that he wasn't going to miss seeing his girl dance.

I wind my way through the dancers until I find an opening, tilt my head back, close my eyes and start to move. My hips sway to the beat and my hands are above my head when I feel bodies close in on me. Hard fingers dig into my hips and another set slides around to cup my ass. Hot breath hits my ear causing my core to clench.

"There's my fucking girl, my Butterfly. No bars to keep me away from you now, angel."

Ash's low, guttural words send a thrill through me. I'm finally dancing for my bar boyfriend again but it's so much better because he's no longer just watching me with desire-filled eyes. This time I get to feel that desire as he grinds his hardness against my ass. My eyes flutter open when I feel a big hot hand drag up the slit of my dress on one side and they meet the icy blues of my Beck.

"Fuck me, darlin' you look like a shiny red apple I want to eat in this dress. You're the best kind of temptation."

I revel in their hot, hard bodies pressed against me as we dance and grind into a panting mess. After a while, Ash steps back and Jude takes his place but he doesn't go far. He watches us with those jade green eyes and they're filled with all the dark, filthy things he's going to do to me as Jude's mouth slides a trail of heat up my neck from my bare shoulder.

"Mmm, baby doll. Not gonna last long here tonight. Need to eat your pussy until I suffocate between your thighs. It's gonna be an all-you-can-eat Savy buffet with all of us filling our plates."

I moan and push my ass back against him as images of all their mouths on me flash through my head. Beck moves even closer so I slide a flat palm down over his chest to his abs and feel them twitch under my hand. He smirks and brings his mouth to the other side of my neck.

"You're so fucking hot, darlin'. We're going to use this tight little body of yours so good when we get home."

I spin between them so Beck's at my back and Jude's pressing against my front, reaching up and back to hook around his neck and say, "Tell me how you'll use me."

Jude runs his tongue over his bottom lip and slides a hot hand into the slit of my dress to wrap around my thigh and Beck tips my chin up as his huge hand grips my throat with just the right pressure to have my heart racing.

"You're going to take all of our cocks, darlin'. We're going to stretch all your pretty little holes at the same time and make it burn so fucking good."

My eyes slide to the right and meet jade green ones that are filled with dark promises and I tremble. Those eyes watch me and caress my body and have wet heat dampening my inner thighs. I fucking love how he watches me. I always have.

I lift my gaze to my final man high above and see him gripping the railing. His fingers flex around it as his eyes burn a path over the three of us moving, grinding to the beat and when he sees me looking back, a sexy smirk crosses his face as he arches a brow as if to ask, 'Are you ready for this, baby girl?' I swallow the moan that wants to fall from my lips because, hell yes, I am.

"I can't wait," I whisper up at Beck. "Take me home. I need you…all of you, right now."

Jude jerks his head at Tate above and I see him disappear and then Ash is next to us tugging on my hand to pull me from the crowd. I spot Stella near one of the bars and send her a small wave that we're leaving. She blows me a kiss and sends me a wink.

The five of us wait together for the valet to bring the SUV around with my men surrounding me in a wall as cameras flash. Beck's hand is on my lower back, Jude and Ash each hold one of my hands and Tate rests a hand on my shoulder. And I smile. Let them look, let them take their pictures, let them see how loved I am.

Ash drives us away with Jude in the front next to him and Tate and Beck on either side of me in the back. My body thrums in anticipation of what's to come and I know I can't wait a minute longer. So I take Tate's hand and rest it on my thigh, hitting him with a desperate look.

"Baby, I ache."

Jude's head whips around from the front seat to my face and then down to where my hand covers Tate's and a wicked grin lights up his face.

"You heard her. My doll aches to be touched, brother. She needs relief."

He bites down on his plush bottom lip and juts his head at Beck.

"Our brother's still recovering, man. You should give him a hand."

I suck in a breath when they both curve toward me and two hot hands slide up the slits in my dress to my inner thighs. Beck brushes against my dampness with the back of his big fingers, causing him to curse.

"Fuck! No underwear, darlin'?"

The other three groan and Ash's eyes meet mine in the rear-view mirror before he reaches up and angles it down.

"Show me."

He demands in a strangled voice that makes me squirm. I drag my dress up over my thighs and lift my ass enough to get it to my waist, exposing myself to all of them. Jude bites on his fist when the passing street lamps show them just how wet I am.

"Fuck me, spread her knees, boys. Show us all that wet pretty pink!"

Tate and Beck follow orders perfectly and hook my knees over theirs exposing me further. I arch my back as the cool air hits me and then moan when two sets of thick fingers slide through my folds.

"Her sad little cunt's weeping because it's empty, brothers. Make it happy," Jude directs them.

Beck latches onto the back of my neck and turns my head to devour my mouth as he rubs my clit. Tate circles my hole and then thrusts a finger up into me. It feels so fucking good that my hips lift, wanting more. Beck tears his mouth from mine and leans back to watch Tate fingering me for a few moments and then tugs the top of my dress down so my breasts spill out.

"Gonna suck on those sweet berry nipples of yours, darlin', while Tate and I fuck your pussy with our fingers. You're going to come so hard all over this seat you'll leave a puddle on the leather."

Yes, fucking yes! I thread my fingers through his hair and drag him down to my chest, crying out when he pulls my nipple deep into his mouth and sucks. My hand slides into Tate's lap and I cup and then squeeze his hard cock through his dress pants and he bites down on my bare shoulder.

They work me up further and further as Jude watches with wide hot eyes until he tells them, "Together. Fuck her pussy together, boys. I want to see it stretch around both your fingers."

I'm a wet mess as my pussy gushes, wanting that. They combine their fingers and slide slowly into my throbbing channel. Four big, rough fingers thrust deep inside again and again sending my head back in ecstasy as my orgasm builds and builds. The car jerks in our lane.

"Jesus, Jude! We're all going to die."

Ash curses, causing Jude to laugh maniacally as he dives between the seats. He's hanging half in the front and half in the back as he buries his face between my spread thighs and lashes my clit with his tongue overtop of the fingers deep inside of me. That's all it takes to send me over the top and my cries ring out as I jerk and thrash against them.

Jude looks up at me with my juices glistening on his chin and lips.

"But what a perfect fucking way to go."

I toss my head back with a laugh even as my channel throbs for more. Jude's eyes track over to my hand clutching Tate through his pants and he reaches for it, covering my fingers with his and moving them to stroke.

"Let's see this cock, doll. Take it out."

I eagerly do as he says but then look up at Tate with concern.

"Is this okay? Are you feeling okay? Any pain?"

He smiles softly at me. "I'm good, baby girl. Don't worry, I know my limits. Now open your pretty mouth and suck on it."

I shift onto my hip to get a better angle to go down and feel Beck cup my ass and then slide his fingers back into my pussy. Jude takes Tate's cock in his hand and fists the base hitting me with glimmering eyes.

"Let me see you suck him like a Slurpee, doll."

Tate moans, "Fuck, Jude, tighter, man."

Jude squeezes Tate's cock and slides his fist up and down as I take the dripping tip into my mouth. I swirl my tongue around it, lapping up the warm precum. Jude uses his free hand to join Beck on my ass and he strokes down between my ass cheeks with a blunt finger circling my tight hole.

"Gonna eat this ass when we get home, baby doll. Stick my tongue right up in it until you're screaming for me to fuck it with my cock. Every fucking hole is getting fucked tonight, baby."

I cry out around Tate's shaft as he thrusts up into my mouth and I've never wanted a drive to go faster or last longer in my life. Tate's fingers make a fist in my hair as he fucks up into my mouth and just as his hot seed hits the back of my throat, my second orgasm hits hard and deep causing me to gag and groan as stars spark in my eyes.

We all jolt as the car comes to a hard stop and then Ash is slamming his door, pulling open the one next to Tate and yanking me out into his arms. I wrap my legs around his waist, put my arms around his neck and hold on tight as he runs us up to the front door and slams me against it.

"Can't wait, Butterfly. Need you on my cock right this fucking second."

He tells me as his hand goes between us and his zipper goes down. He jerks me higher against the door and then I feel the large blunt head of his cock shove into me.

"Fuck, fuck, yes! Fuck me, Ash. I need you! Hard, do it hard and fast." I beg.

He gives me everything I want right there against our front door. Jude and Beck join us on either side.

They take my legs from around his waist and spread them out so they're supporting me with hands under my ass and thighs. Ash rears back, looks down at where we're joined and uses his thumbs to spread my pussy lips open. His thumbs drag down on either side of my clit and then he slams back into me deep and hard like a fucking machine.

I cry his name out into the night and Jude slaps a hand over my mouth with a laugh. Both he and Beck bend forward and suck on my nipples and as if they planned it ahead of time, bite down simultaneously, causing me to buck against Ash's thrusts and scream my orgasm out against Jude's hand. Ash jerks inside me and I feel his heat spread through me before it starts to trickle out.

I go loose and limp and they transfer me to Beck's arms while they get the door open and the alarm shut off. My head bobs against Beck's chest sleepily as he carries me deeper into the house and then downstairs. A soft light comes on as he lays me out on a bed. I go up on my elbows and take a look around at what used to be a theater room. I laugh when I see the soundproofing panels on the walls and the massive platform bed I'm lying on.

Jude crawls onto the bed toward me and then strips the red dress up and over my head with a grin.

"You like? We had it made just for our family bonding time. Can't have little ears hearing you scream, doll."

And then he yanks my knees apart and shoves his face into my pussy. My hands go to his hair and pull him back with a laugh.

"Jude! Let me clean off first!"

He licks his lips and shakes his head.

"Nuh-uh, this is my favorite, I love you all sloppy and filthy. My tongue's gonna clean it all up so we can dirty you back up again." He tells me and then dives back in, licking up all of Ash and my mess.

He strokes me with his tongue again and again as my eyes watch the others strip down. They climb on the bed around us on their knees with fists wrapped around their cocks and stare down at my body with heat-filled eyes. It awakens a dirty animal inside of me and I unleash it with my voice.

"I need a cock in my pussy and one down my throat!"

Four groans ring out, making me smirk smugly before I'm dragged higher up the bed with Beck settling behind me against the headboard. He pulls me between his legs and up his chest so my back is against him and orders Jude in a growl, "Put my cock in her and then lick us."

My head goes dizzy at his hot as fuck command and Jude's right there getting to work as Tate and Ash slide in on either side of us to watch. I press my chin on my chest to watch Jude's ink-covered fingers stroke Beck's angry red cock a few times, squeezing the head of it in his hand first before pressing it back against my heat and pushing it into my drenched core. Beck nudges me higher and thrusts up a few times, stretching me out in the best possible way. Jude drags his fingers through my pussy down to where the cock fucks into me with an approving hum and then settles on his stomach between our legs.

Ash and Tate grab my thighs and spread me even further, their hot palms squeezing me. I feel worshiped as they all gaze down at my pussy. Ash grabs Jude by the hair and pushes his face against us.

"I want to see that tongue on them. Lick her cream off his cock as he fucks it out of her."

Oh God, oh God, Jude's tongue swipes over my clit and down to lick Beck's shaft as he thrusts in and out of me and it has my channel pulsing and squeezing around that cock.

I could watch this all fucking night but Tate lifts my chin to look at him. My eyes scan over the cock in his hand, up over his abs, stalling out at the ugly scar on his chest. I tense up but he wraps a hand around my throat making me look higher and promises,

"I'm okay, baby. I promise, I'm okay. Let me show you. Let me fuck that pretty mouth of yours again."

I nod my agreement at the reassurance in his eyes and open my mouth. His hands come up to either side of my head and hold me firm as he thrusts in until he hits the back of my throat. I wrap my lips around his shaft and swallow down against him causing him to grunt. Tate shows me just how fine he is as he picks up speed, fucking my mouth with abandon as Beck's cock pulses against my womb and Jude licks everything that spills out away.

Tears streak down my face as pleasure courses through me. Every touch, every lick, every thrust, rolls my orgasm into another as these men ruin my body. Beck licks, kisses, and sucks up my neck telling me how perfect I am and how much he loves me.

"Hop off his dick, doll. I want you riding Ash's now."

Tate pulls from my mouth and with another sizzling kiss, Beck lifts me off his lap and Ash takes his place. He turns me around so our chests are pressed together and I'm straddling him. Jude moves up onto his knees and presses against my back, gripping my ass. Ash pulls my bottom lip down with his thumb before sliding it into my mouth. I suck down on it and drag my teeth over his knuckle.

"You ready to fly, Butterfly?"

I release his thumb with a pop and grin.

"Take me to heaven, bar boyfriend."

Jude lifts my hips and slams me back down on Ash's dick and I see stars. I ride and roll against him, taking my pleasure as Jude's cock slides through my ass cheeks. He palms my breasts and lifts them in offering to Beck and Tate to suck on.

Fuck, I want it, I want all of it so damn bad. I ache for these men in a way I didn't know was possible. Jude pulls back and drags his rough hands down my back to cup my ass and spread my cheeks. I moan, thinking I know where this is going, and push the men licking my nipples to the side so I can bend forward to offer my ass to him. I want his cock in me too. I want to feel all of them in me.

Jude chuckles darkly and slaps my ass. The zip of pain rubbed away with a soothing hand.

"Not yet, baby doll. We're going to fill you a different way first."

My brows furrow at that, not understanding until I feel the head of his cock push against Ash's and slowly slide into me next to it. The burn of the stretch has me gasping but Beck's there, sliding his hand between Ash and my body to play with my clit. He circles it, flicks it, and I start to relax again.

"Fuck, Jude! I can feel your piercings pressing into my dick." Ash groans.

Jude laughs, "Don't worry, Savy and I will lick the indents better when we're done here."

Tate makes a choked noise so I look over my shoulder in worry but find him jacking into his hand with his blazing eyes locked onto Jude's cock as it slips inside of my pussy, snug up against Ash's.

"Fucking perfection." He breathes out roughly. "Baby girl, you look so fucking beautiful taking their cocks together. Your pussy's magic. It's stretching and sucking them in, begging for more." His eyes lift to meet mine and go hard and intense. "Open your fucking mouth and take mine too. We're all going to fuck you at once."

I swallow hard, feeling so damn full with two cocks inside me but Beck strokes my clit faster causing me to cry out and Tate slides between my lips until he hits the back of my throat. Jude and Ash move as one, fucking me in tandem and the world fades away. It's all pleasure sparking through me and there's no way it could get any better.

I must say it out loud around Tate's cock because Beck growls, "Yes it can."

His hand disappears from my pussy causing me to whine but Ash's replaces it and then I feel cool liquid on my ass as it slides between my cheeks. My eyes flutter open again and I pull my mouth off of Tate to turn my head. Beck kneels behind Jude, reaches around him, and drags his fingers through the lube to massage my asshole. He circles it a few times and then presses his finger in to the first knuckle. I moan loudly the deeper he goes into me. Two cocks in my pussy and now Beck's second finger slides into my ass and starts to pump. I've never felt so full before and it's overwhelming. I don't think I can take much more as my body's rocked again and again by them but Tate drags my face back to him and presses the head of his cock against my lips.

"All of us, baby girl. Every fucking hole!"

He squeezes my jaw until I open my mouth and fucks in hard and fast. I'm a whimpering, moaning mess as I take everything they have and the orgasm barrels down on me so fucking hard and fast my vision whites out and I scream around his cock deep in my throat.

"Fuck, fuck, fuck! She's squeezing us so fucking tight!"

Jude stutters as both he and Ash throb inside of me and their cum floods my channel and drips out of me and down my legs. I can't think, I can't breathe. I'm lost to the pleasure that's destroying my body and mind.

Jude slips out of me and then Beck lifts me off of Ash and pulls me down the bed. He barks, "Tate, on your back. It's our turn to stretch this perfect pussy."

I roll my head and whine, "Too much, too, much!"

But Beck just laughs and spins me around until I'm straddling Tate. Beck pushes my upper body down against him until I'm draped bonelessly against his chest.

"You can give us more, darlin'. You can take us all."

I murmur a yes as Tate sweeps my hair to the side and kisses down my face to my lips.

"You're such a good girl, baby. You take our cocks perfectly. You can take more. I promise you'll love it. Let us fuck you again. Let us love you."

He strokes his hands down my body as my hips start rolling over his cock sliding it against my oversensitive pussy. It's too much and not enough at the same time.

"Please, please, fuck me again. I need you, I need more."

His first stroke into me is slow and easy. I'm so soft and wet from all the cum inside of me and the orgasms, I don't even feel the stretch of him until he pops his hips and drags against that spot inside that brings the sparkles back to my eyes. I tilt my ass up and match him stroke for stroke, my fingers digging into his arms. Beck squares up behind me, feet on the floor, and drags his large, blunt tip down my ass.

"Yes! Do it! Please!" I beg as he lines himself up with my ass and starts to slowly push inside. Suddenly, my drowsiness disappears and everything goes hot and bright. I push back against his cock as Tate thrusts up until he fills me completely. Jesus! This is a different fullness than having Ash and Jude inside me at once, a different kind of fullness that I crave more of.

"Harder!"

I beg as they rock into me, slow and smooth. I want hard, I want fast, I want every-fucking-thing they've got!

"You heard her, brothers. Give our girl what she wants! Fuck that pussy and ass until she screams." Jude barks.

He presses up against Tate's side and pulls my hand off his arm to his mouth to kiss my knuckles. He runs his lips over my nails and admires the candy apple red polish and grins.

"Pretty, I was just thinking that I want my cock wrapped in red, doll."

He moves up higher beside us and wraps my fingers around his cock and then grabs Tate's and covers mine with his. Tate moans and threads his fingers between mine and together we jack Jude off while two cocks plow my holes. As the wave crests, I turn my head and meet hot jade eyes as Ash moves in to fuck my mouth with his lips and tongue and together we all fall.

I lay limply in the center of the bed as warm damp cloths wash away the mess and rough hands pet and stroke me as they whisper how much they love their baby. My eyes flutter closed and I check in with myself. Mentally, I'm wide open, completely bare and exposed to them. The cage, the wall, all my masks - are gone - burned away by their love.

EPILOGUE

Five years later…

The crowd in the stands are on their feet as the clock runs down, screaming their heads off for him to go, go, go. Jude caught the ball seconds ago and is dodging, twisting, and spinning on his feet to make the last points we need to win the game and take the Superbowl home. And what a win it would be for him. He's already announced that this will be his last game, ready to retire from the sport and join Tate in the kid's football training club that he's built.

My gaze roams the executive box with a smile as I take in all the cheering people I love. Beck has Tanner in a death grip as they lean forward against the rail screaming for Jude. Stella bounces one of my three-year-old twin daughters on her hip as she claps her tiny hands for her daddy on the field. Mark rocks the other one, soothing her as the loud noises overwhelm her and Tate slides up behind me and cups my growing belly with baby number three inside. A baby boy that's kicking my bladder like he's practicing to be the next pro placekicker.

Jude makes the touchdown and the noise goes nuclear. I can feel the vibrations through my feet as the stadium goes wild around us.

I lean back into Tate with a wide smile and then tip my head back to look up at him and ask, "Do you miss it, baby?"

He presses a kiss on the top of my head.

"Only a little and only at times like this but otherwise, no. I have everything I need right here, baby girl. I love my life."

I smile up at him and then pull my eyes back to the field where Jude's being pummeled by his teammates piling on in celebration. I couldn't agree with Tate more. I love our life. With Sevan sold and me free to choose my path, I turned to my first passion, literature. I've built a small publishing house with authors I love and believe in and Butterfly Ink has just had our latest release hit the New York Times bestseller list at a respectable number thirty-four. It's a huge win for my small start-up and puts my authors and company on the map of the publishing world.

Mark brings over Poppy as she reaches for me. Her white-blond hair clings to her tear-streaked, flushed face and I can tell from the glassiness of her sky-blue eyes she's ready for bed. She wraps her tiny legs around me above my baby bump and presses her warm, damp face into my neck as I soothe her back. She's a quiet, reserved little thing. She reminds me of how I was as a child. It's the polar opposite of her twin, Piper. That girl has all of her daddy's traits. She's wild, passionate, and fearless.

We knew almost right away after their births that Jude was the daddy but all my men are their fathers and love them with their whole souls. I'm pretty sure the one currently stomping on my bladder is Ash's. The dates line up with a drunken weekend we spent together at a rental cabin we snuck off to. It involved a private hot tub and the loss of our deposit when we broke some of the furniture during our wild lovemaking. The tears that filled his eyes when I told him made me fall even more in love with him.

My ribs creak as the baby stretches against his sister pressing against my side and I almost reconsider the promise I made to them all about having two more kids but when Tate lifts the now sleeping Poppy off of me to snuggle her and Beck looks back with love filled eyes at me, I know I'll never deny them anything.

He waves me over to the railing as Jude's voice rings out through the speakers in the stadium calling my name. I groan at whatever idiot gave him a microphone as I take my place in full view of the crowds looking this way. Ash is wading through the crowd of players on the field to head him off when his voice booms out.

"There she is! My baby doll! We did it, baby. We kicked their asses! Grab the kids, we're gonna go home and celebrate with pizza and then I'm gonna plow your field with my monster trac…"

Thank goodness someone has the sense to cut the feed before he could finish that sentence. He's been talking about buying land after he retires and trying his hand at farming. We all know it's just a Jude ploy to make ridiculous sexual innuendos. He's taken to calling his cock his monster tractor and telling me all the ways he wants to plow me with it. He also told me he wants to wear Carhartt's while he plants his 'seeds' in me. I fucking love him with every fiber of my being.

The crowd still caught the gist of it and cheers even louder, causing a deep red blush to climb up my neck and flush my cheeks. It doesn't stop the huge smile from spreading over my face as I blow him an exaggerated kiss though. One of the other players passes him the huge trophy and he holds it up to me with one hand and points at the top of it while wiggling his brows.

I throw my head back with a laugh. I know exactly what he's doing. This morning he said he was going to win, bring that trophy home and make me ride it, rubbing my clit all over it until I came. I embrace his crazy by matching it, lift my hands and pull my fingers toward me in a bring it on gesture. My baby's mouth drops open and then he's whooping and tossing the trophy to the next player. He races across the field, climbs up and over the boundary wall, and dashes up the stairs. Fans reach out and pat his back, and tug on his jersey but he swerves and jumps and keeps on climbing until he's right under the box.

His golden eyes flash with delight when I lean over the railing as far as my bump will allow and grin down at him.

He smirks up at me and asks, "You playing me, doll?"

And I tell him exactly what he wants to hear.

"No, baby, but I'll play with you, every day…forever."

The End

Please take a second to click a rating and if you can take a minute to review it would mean the world! Thanks, Reese

Looking for more? Sign up to my newsletter to be notified of new releases!

www.reeserivers.com

PREVIEW
Falls Like Rain RH

Rain

People say fate's funny but she's not. She's a cunt. That bitch will string you along, showing you glimpses of everything you think you want, lead you down the path of all your dreams and then laugh when she cuts your throat and circles you back to where you started from. Like I said, cunt.

I cringe at the vulgar word that comes so easily to my mind. That's not who I am anymore. I worked damn hard to leave that raw, untamed girl behind. I swear, the closer I got to where I began, the more that girl pushed back in.

I stare through the windshield of my car at the single-wide trailer lit up by my headlights. I've been frozen here behind the wheel since I drove up the dirt lane twenty minutes ago. I can't bring myself to shut the car off and get out. It's like if I don't leave the car, none of this is really happening. The only thing I see as I stare at the rundown trailer that I lived in for seventeen years and three hundred and sixty-four days is me slipping out of the cracked bedroom window. I snuck out with an envelope of cash and a backpack full of clothes hours before the clock ticked over to my eighteenth birthday.

My eyes slide away from the trailer and across the fallow field, tracing the path I took that night to where my best girlfriend waited for me in her rusted-out Dodge Neon that was held together by duct tape and primer paint. That car held together enough for her to drive me the hour to the closest town that had a bus going through it.

I ran to protect them. Hoping for something more, something…better. And I forced myself to not look back. I held true to that for eight fucking years. I found different, I thought I found better - and then that cunt laughed and laughed and took it all away with one phone call.

My fingers squeeze the steering wheel tighter, making the diamond ring on my finger pinch my skin. I drop my eyes to it in the dim light just as a flash of lightning rips across the sky making it shine mockingly at me and wish I had left it on the counter of the condo. The cold rock on my finger was supposed to represent the next stage of my life, my future. But that phone call sent me to Jason's office in search of comfort and support.

What I got instead was a full view of him slamming his dick into his assistant while she was bent over his desk. When he looked up and spotted me watching, his eyes went colder than I'd ever seen them before. He looked annoyed, even frustrated that I was interrupting him. There was absolutely no guilt in his eyes as he pumped a few more times into her to finish himself off.

He caught me just as the elevator doors opened and grabbed my wrist so hard that I have a pretty ring of black and blue bruises circling it. My throat was locked up in a double knot of grief from the phone call telling me that my father was dead and losing what I thought was my future with a man who loved me. He squeezed my wrist harder with a jerk making me look up at him.

"Go home and wait for me there, Rain. We'll discuss this when I get there later."

I yanked my arm trying to get free but he just squeezed harder, making the delicate bones grind together painfully.

His jaw clenched and his tone was filled with warning when he told me, "You will want to consider very carefully any rash or knee-jerk reactions you might want to have in regards to what you just saw. It changes nothing."

He stared hard into my eyes and then dropped my arm gesturing me towards the waiting elevator.

As the doors closed between us, I took a good long look at him because he was wrong. What I saw changed everything and there was no going back. I had felt like a zombie leaving his office building and getting a cab to our condo. I felt nothing but emptiness and numbness when I walked through the ultra-modern space on the top floor with sweeping views of the city.

Clothes were thrown in heaps into suitcases, bathroom toiletries swept into a bulging bag and every last trace of me was removed from that condo by the time I called the doorman up to carry it all down to the underground parking garage and into my car. I was robotic as I opened my banking app and transferred out the money I had contributed to it, leaving his much bigger amount behind.

I didn't want a cent of his money. I didn't even feel a hitch of sadness when I sent the wedding planner an email telling her to cancel everything and that the wedding was off. I drove away from him, away from my life and away from a broken future - all the way back to here where I had started and where I had run from all those years ago. Maybe that's who I am, a runner. Maybe that's all I'll ever be, a woman who runs from everything.

I stare at that ring on my finger as the storm moves closer and lightning flashes across the sky until I can't take it anymore. As thunder cracks and rumbles, I let it all out and I scream and scream and scream. When my voice is gone and I can't scream anymore, I push open the car door and walk halfway to the rickety steps of the trailer but my feet come to a stop. I can't. I can't go in there yet and face the emptiness, the memories.

The hair lifts on the back of my neck when I hear a horse whinny in the distance from behind me. Goosebumps race across my skin. I know, even before I turn, what I'll see. With the storm building closer and closer I turn and face the direction where my heart used to live and I wait. Lightning flashes and lights up the heavens again and there they are. Outlined on the hill are three men sitting on horses looking my way.

We stare at each other across the distance until the lightning dies and drops us back into darkness. That's when I dive back into my car and quickly drive away because I finally feel something. I feel everything - and the regret choking me now tastes a lot like fear. I drive back to town to find a room for the night and I swear I can hear that cunt, Fate, laughing in the storm.

Chance

Luke throws tack down hard on the kitchen table scratching the old wood even more than it already is. I don't bother looking up from the dredges of my coffee cup. After giving up even trying to sleep, I'm already a full pot in even though the sun is just now rising.

I doubt any of us got much sleep last night after seeing her standing in front of her dad's beat-up trailer. We had been out wrangling a few mothers and calves who were too stupid to come in from the storm that was brewing when I saw the headlights flashing down the long driveway to the trailer.

I don't know why it was a surprise to see her there. We knew she'd come back to handle her daddy's affairs but it still felt like a mule kick to my gut to see her that close after so long. Eight fucking years without one damn word from her had hardened and withered the place she used to own inside me, leaving nothing but a thick layer of hurt covered over by anger. Judging by the scowl on Luke's face, he felt the same. Rex, well, he passed through the house last night long enough to snag a bottle of whiskey and then disappear somewhere back out into the storm.

Luke grunts as he drops into his chair across from me and drags a hand down his face. I lean back in my chair and just wait, knowing it'll take him a minute to build up to asking. He's always been slow to speak his thoughts, a product of never quite feeling like he belonged with us. Luke's time in the Marines burned away the sweetness he had as a boy and gave him a harder edge but that uncertainty never quite went away. Especially when he was dealing with strong emotions.

He fidgets with the tack he brought in to repair and finally tosses it back down on the table with a deep sigh.

"Do we have to see her? I doubt she'll be here for long. Can we just…not?"

I rub my mouth to stall, hating her a little bit more for coming back and cracking open his wounds. I curse under my breath before answering him.

"We do, but you don't have to talk to her. We'll stand at the back for the service and duck out as soon as it's over. We have to pay our respects to her daddy, it's only fitting."

His brow furrows and I see a glimpse of the sweet, sad boy he used to be but then he gives a sharp nod as his face hardens to the man he's become. He sweeps the bridle back up before walking out of the house again. I circle the rim of my empty coffee cup with one finger as memories of the aftermath of her leaving pass through my mind.

And then I pick up that mug and throw it at the wall. Fuck her for leaving and fuck her even more for coming back.

I allow myself a few more minutes of brooding before I push to my feet and clean the mess I made. Rain probably won't be here for more than the few days it'll take to bury her dad and settle the paperwork but I have a gut feeling she'll leave a bigger mess behind when she leaves again. A mess I'll also have to clean up. I scrub my tired face again and scoop up my keys, heading to the door. No point putting it off, she's here and it'll be better to face it head-on.

The drive to town is just long enough to give my tired brain time to remember. I don't let myself think about the sweet times of before, I only focus on the wreckage of the after.

The day Rex finally accepted that she was gone and not coming back. How he slipped away in the night with only a brief note to say goodbye. The years of abuse he put his body through in the reckless pursuit to drown the pain of losing her. And how he only came back when his body couldn't take the beatings anymore. The way he self-medicates now with the bottle and blunts.

I remember driving Luke to the bus after he enlisted and all the nights I laid awake terrified he wouldn't make it home. Always afraid he'd take a bullet or a bomb in some arid desert country we had no business being in. I remember the sheer relief of him finally coming home for good after his last deployment and then the despair of seeing the haunted look in his eyes that never quite goes away.

I remember being the last one left on the ranch. Trying every day to please that bastard until we almost came to blows and I finally left myself. The endless nights of cramming knowledge into my brain until I passed the bar and then the call that brought me back to take over the ranch. And every damn day of it feeling like half of my soul was missing with everyone I loved gone.

I pull my truck up in front of the diner and tilt my head back, looking for a little peace from my thoughts for a few minutes. Finally, I give up and drag both my hands through my hair before getting out and heading inside for my breakfast.

Dolly, the owner nods her good morning as she reaches for the coffee pot. Clint, her husband and fry cook, lifts a hand in greeting through the food window. I settle into my regular booth at the back of the diner and flip the old chipped coffee mug over just as Dolly reaches me to pour.

"Mornin', darling. Clint will have your regular out in no time. Give a holler when you want a top off."

I shoot her a wink as she sways back to the counter, the pink polyester fabric of her uniform strained by her ample curves and her big brown curls locked on top of her head by a cloud of Aqua Net. I can never smell that scent without thinking of Dolly and smiling.

By the time I'm through with my meal, the diner is full-up with patrons. I've kept my head down since I sat, in no state of mind for casual chit chat but the next time the chimes ring out over the door, a hush seems to settle over the crowd. I know she's walked in before I even lift my head.

My stomach churns and my skin feels too tight before my eyes even land on her back. She's waiting at the counter as Dolly fills a to-go cup for her. My knuckles whiten around the edge of the table and even though I told Luke we didn't have to talk to her, my feet decide otherwise. I scan the sleek, smooth fall of blond hair I used to love to touch when it was wild with waves and the classy linen skirt that does nothing to hide her mouth-watering curves.

I move up right behind her and hear her gasp under her breath, "That son of a bitch."

It makes me smirk until I look over her shoulder and spot the ring of dark bruises around her wrist and the flashy, oversized rock on her finger as she holds out her bank card.

COMING SOON!

FALLS LIKE RAIN

Also By Reese Rivers

There's ninety-two dollars and fifty-seven cents hidden in a Ziploc bag in the lining of the couch along with a double stack of polaroid pictures that might buy me some time. Every person who has met my husband thinks he's the most charming man and would never believe what he does to me behind these four walls. And now, I see my five-year-old daughter's arm in a cast. Something I vow never to let happen again.

Ninety-two dollars and fifty-seven cents. It's not enough, but it will have to be.

This sweet and steamy, contemporary romance standalone has references to domestic abuse that may cause triggers. The main heroine

finds love with all three men as they heal each other and become a family.

On the run, living in their car as winter sets in, Avery will do whatever it takes to hide from a monster and keep her daughter safe. One good deed on a snowy night changes everything.

Three former military men and one German Shepherd with their own damage take the mother and daughter in. They fall hard for Avery and Chloe and will burn the world down to keep them safe.

Easton – carries the guilt of failure at losing half his unit in their last engagement. He sees too many parallels to his own childhood trauma with Avery and Chloe. His honor demands that he cares for and protects them. He fights his attraction to Avery with an iron will.

Zack – The charming playboy had his self-esteem gutted by the scars his body carries and the loss of his leg. One tiny girl has him changing his perspective on his injuries. Avery sees the man not the injury and the hole inside him slowly begins to fill with a love he never thought he'd have a chance at again.

Ryker – His sheer size and bulk intimidate and keep a safe distance between him and others. A man of few words, his main forms of communication are long drawn-out growls and grunts. The tiny wisp of a girl cracks all his armor with her sweetness and her mother feels like a missing piece of his soul when she's in his arms. When he finds the man who hurt them, he will annihilate him in the most painful way possible.

Kanga (dog) – The lady makes his pack happy and her female pup reminds him that there's fun to be had, dimming the memories of bullets and bombs that took him and his pack out of the fight.

Dying To Love

662 – Days since the dead rose up
413 – Days since I've spoken to another living human
4 – Men who have climbed my fence looking for safety
1 – Last chance for Love

Kelsey survived the start of the apocalypse and thrived in the new world with help from her friends but now they're gone. Alone for over a year and mentally broken with high anxiety, she pushes through every day trying to find the will to keep going. Until three sweet, sexy men and one hot a**hole climb her fence looking for sanctuary.

With her best friend, Tara, haunting her with outrageous antics, she needs to decide if she wants to keep dying a little bit day by day or if she can grab on to what these sexy men offer her and maybe find love.

Also, zombies make a few cameos.

This isn't a blood and gore zombie novel. It's full of comedy, overprotective men that just want to take care of her, and a ton of sexy steam that happens behind a set of double fences.

Enjoy this great standalone!

Time After Time

A Time Travel RH 3 Book Series

How do you survive time travel to 17th-century France…while wearing a bathrobe…with nothing to help you but an iPhone? How do you avoid being burnt at the stake as a witch for possessing that 'magical' evil iPhone?

Start by being rescued by 4 hot AF men. Accept that vampires and wolf shifters are real and then make peace with the fact that you can have them all.

Eden Kelly's life is in ruins. Traumatized and alone, she struggles to keep living every day until she stumbles through a magic mirror that sends her hurtling back in time to 1667.

Sebastian, Luca, Finn, and Cade are completely captivated by the woman that appears in front of them as they go into battle. Her modern ways, smart, sassy mouth, and stunning beauty have them entranced and filled with desire. They recognize the damaged soul and anguish she tries to hide as they all have similar pain that they live with. It has them aching to tend, care and soothe her as she unknowingly does the same for them.

Can a modern woman find love and happiness with these men or will time end all things and suck her back to her desolate modern life?

Get started on your next great series with Book 1 in the Time After Time series!

Catch Me

YA Post Apocalyptic Titles Written as Theresa Shaver

The Stranded Series

Land – A Stranded Novel, Book One

Sea – A Stranded Novel, Book Two

Home - A Stranded Novel, Book Three

City Escape – A Stranded Novel, Book Four

Frozen – A Stranded Novel Book Five

Iced – A Stranded Novel Book Six

The Endless Winter Series

Snow & Ash – An Endless Winter Novel, Book One

Rain & Ruin – An Endless Winter Novel, Book Two

Sun & Smoke – An Endless Winter Novel, Book Three

Fire & Fury – An Endless Winter Novel, Book Four

Scorched – A Dry Earth Novel

The Flare Series

The Journey – A Flare Novel, Book One

The Line – A Flare Novel, Book Two

The Bridge – A Flare Novel, Book Three

Printed in Great Britain
by Amazon

60085875R00224